# I Met An Angel

To Ken,

Thank you for visiting my table at the Community Fair.

I look forward to working with you!

Omar

ISBN: 1-59109-568-9

Printed in Canada

ANGELO
OMAR

# I MET AN ANGEL

A NOVEL

2003

# I Met An Angel

# TABLE OF CONTENTS

ACKNOWLEDGMENTS TO ALL THOSE WHO INSPIRED ME INCLUDING:

ALL MIGHTY ALLAH (GOD)
(and those who work in His name)

MY GRANDMOTHER
MILDRED WASHINGTON

MY LOVING FRIEND
IMANI AMOUR
(and her family)

MY MOTHER
MRS. IRENE DASHER

EDWARD ANDERSON
FOR COUNSEL AND EDITING SERVICES
ANDREA ROBINSON - TYPIST

JOSEPH LEE WASHINGTON
MYKE WASHINGTON
MARY LEIGH NELSON
TARIQ YASIN WASHINGTON
MALCOLM ROAN
ASIA IMANI MUHAMMAD
OMAR KARRIEM MUHAMMAD

(and the rest of my immediate and extended family)

*This Book Is Dedicated To The Angels Forever In My Life:*

*My Grandmother*

*Mildred Washington*

*&*

*My Loving Friend*

*Imani Amour*

#

*(They Will Always Live Within Me)*

# INTRODUCTION

***

Truth is such a powerful thing. Truth enlightens us and challenges us to change. Truth dispels falsehood as light dispels darkness. Truth, like light has the power to cause motion. As light strikes the earth at it equator causing the earth to turn, it shows us that if truth strikes us in the right place and hits the right nerve, it will also cause movement and change. If truth hits you, I mean really, really hits you, then there must be change.

This book is designed for just that purpose, for I am not writing this book for merely entertainment purposes. I am not writing this book to satisfy any vain desires within myself. I am writing this book to challenge each of us to move towards the things that are right and to leave the negative energy alone and begin moving toward positive energy.

There is a saying that goes: "Be careful how you entertain strangers, for you could be entertaining Angels, unaware". This is so true and I believe that many times we miss our own blessings by not paying attention to "strangers" that cross our paths.

It must be understood, that the same person may not necessarily be an "Angel" to every other person that they communicate with, but some of the things they say are tailor-made just for you.

So, I use "Angel" not just in the universal sense of the word but also in the individualized sense.

Think about that old lady or old man that you may have had a conversation with in the supermarket, in the park, at work or anywhere else. Now think about those pearls of wisdom they may have provided in a short conversation. What if you decided not to talk to them that day?

If you've ever started a sentence by saying.... "An old man once told me....", then you know what I'm talking about. Sometimes even children are the bearers of refreshing and rejuvenating words. I remember the feeling that came over me one day when my daughter approached me and candidly asked.... Daddy, are you happy? The question surprised me and also challenged me to think deeply. My spirit was eventually renewed by just the thought of my daughter asking me such a question.

You may actually experience many different things during your reading of this book. You may find that you will dig deeply into your own spiritual thoughts. You may also find yourself reflecting on your own past and looking at some of the influences that were both prominent and intricate in your life. You may then find yourself smiling or even laughing as you visualize some of my life's experiences and reminiscing about your own. I am very hopeful that you have these experiences as you read. I am hopeful that you will have the ability to examine your current spiritual, mental, moral and physical condition and weigh it against integrity, character and truth.

I am also hopeful that you will be able to gain valuable lessons from the words provided that you can utilize in your present and future relationships. If this happens, then the words that I have written will transcend the pages they are written on and they become alive. This book can be a valuable tool to recapture something that we were all born with – SUBMISSION.

No individual is really produced and placed here by accident. The *act* of producing a child is not an accident. The *result* of the act that brings a child into existence may in some cases be called an accident but in reality, it was just poor planning or lack of responsible behavior.

Everyone has a distinct purpose in life. Some people come into the realization of that purpose and others never do. In some rare cases the power of the One God or the collective energy in the universe, is actively involved to control the destiny of a particular person or situation. When this happens, and the individual is on a journey sometimes referred to as a "rendezvous with destiny" and they are the bearers of a Divine message they can best be described as Angels even though they may not be totally aware of the level they have been elevated to. They will likely know that they are blessed but they may not know the full scope of their mission.

SOMETIMES OTHERS RECOGNIZE MORE ABOUT YOU THAN YOU RECOGNIZE IN YOURSELF!

# I.
# HOW ANGELS ARRIVE

***

My world had crumbled as if it were struck by a terrible earthquake. The clean, crispness in the air somehow quickly turned stale. The brightness of this clear, sunny spring day in April was suddenly irrelevant. How could it be that dreams and aspirations so great could be obliterated in the blink of an eye?

The more I live, the more I see our lives as a predetermined spiral of activity. Sometimes we spiral upwards and sometimes downward. Our ultimate destiny is already determined and as we live on, we must continue to ride that predetermined spiral or path. When someone comes into your life, and your spirals meet, it is not by accident. In some rare cases, the person who spirals into our lives is so enriched with spiritual energy and purpose that they can be best described as an "ANGEL".

Those of us on the receiving end of such spiritual enlightenment must have the vision and intelligence to first recognize who they are and then have the wisdom and understanding to discern why they came to us.

It is actually the dynamics of the histories of both people involved that brings about a merger with such heightened spirituality. I will attempt to provide the reader with some of my own history in order that you may better understand the type of person I am which may help clarify why I was visited by a very special spiritual being. Change can only occur when there is enough energy and force to bring about that change. The energy is produced by the conditions surrounding various subjects. Altering the conditions, of course, may produce many different changes. We have so many different thoughts going through our minds simultaneously, that it is sometimes confusing to try and grasp how a certain change came about in our lives yet it was the development of our own thoughts that could provide the required energy to produce a change. The scripture says that God will never change the condition of a people until they change it themselves. When we change our thoughts we can actually bring people and things into our reality. This is the basis of the phrase… "ask and it shall be given".

When we ask for things from the heart and we put that energy out into the universe we will get results. Those results can be positive or negative depending upon the state of our heart and our intentions. We sometimes get the answer to our yearning in the form of a person who carries in them the answer to needs. In some cases these occurrences are hardly even noticeable while others carry such impact that one or all parties involved have a life long impression of the incident or meeting or interlude.

When the culmination of the events result in divine revelation and spiritual growth, then you should recognize that an Angel has indeed visited you.

This is my story of an Angel that came to me on a cool, sunny day of October 22, 2001. I was representing the City of Newark's Purchasing Division at a vendor's conference sponsored by the University of Medicine and Dentistry held at the New Jersey Performing Arts Center (NJPAC) in Newark, New Jersey. It was a typical vendor's conference with many companies, public and private who were present, set up with display tables, promoting their particular interests and engaging in conversations with the many vendors who milled around the open area stopping from table to table gathering as much information as they could.

As the pace slowed down and the attendees prepared for the soon to come luncheon that followed in the upper level, I looked over and saw Imani Amour. Imani is a person from my hometown of Plainfield, New Jersey, which is a typical small urban inner city that is surrounded by suburbs. Deeply touched by the "Black Riots" and rebellion of the 1960's, I can still vaguely remember when the military tanks were rolling through the streets and we were told to stay indoors and away from the windows. Plainfield is sometimes referred to as "Peyton Place" because so many people who reside there are either related or know each other and word travels fast throughout the city.

I now reside in Newark, but if I wanted to know about anything going on in Plainfield, I could simply call my mother, who now lives in Georgia, my cousin April or one of my other family members, and get the story. It's just that type of city, but I still love it. I really enjoyed growing up there on both the east and west sides of the city, but I left in 1983 while still a young man because I felt I needed a change and to broaden my horizons. Besides, the move was all a part of my predetermined spiral of activity that would eventually lead me directly to the spiraled path of my Angel.

## 2.
## THE VILLAGE THAT RAISED ME

***

I was the product of a divided home, and was a very young, two or three years of age when my parents were separated. My father, Joseph Theodore Washington, had a total of eleven children (at my last count) including the five children that he and my mother had together. My other siblings from various mothers are Melvin, Kyle, Rita, Charles, Travis, and Tracy. After my parents were separated, I didn't see my mother, Irene Hall (now remarried and known as Irene Dasher) or my younger brother and sister, Michael and Mary Leigh, who lived with my mother, much at all even though we were all in the same city. I never even met my mother's mother.

My father got custody of the three oldest children and my mother got the two youngest children. So, Isha, Joey and myself headed to Hillcrest Avenue with my father, to live with him and my grandparents while Michael and Mary Leigh went with my mother. The highlight of my days back then most likely consisted of just making it back and forth to Emerson School everyday where I was attended Kindergarten, while Isha and Joey attended Cook School.

I was too young to really think deeply about our domestic situation but it did seem a little strange, even back then. I eventually grew up with the question that many children unfortunately grow up with... *"what really happened?"*

Single parents have to use their imaginations sometimes when they want to continue having a social life. I remember once when we were still very young, that my father had a date and couldn't find anyone to watch my brother, sister, or myself so he took us along with him to the drive-in movie. I remember just before getting up to the booth where you pay for the movie, my father turning around and telling us to get down on the floor, then covering our heads with a blanket. I wasn't sure why this tactic was being used. I was too young to think it through back then. In retrospect, it was either that you had to pay by the number of heads in the car and he was avoiding payment, or because it was an X rated film and no children were allowed. It was a movie called the "Valley of the Dolls". I guess single fathers, like single mothers, have to improvise too.

I grew up with a grandmother who was very domestic and caring. She was a nurse for Muhlenburg Hospital for about thirty-seven years. She cared for people regularly at work but did not express or share love physically, in the form of hugs or kisses at home to us, her grandchildren. I didn't understand or think about it much back then but, like they say, you can't give what you don't receive.

Even still, I knew that she loved us dearly, by the way she kept us clean and cooked our oatmeal in the morning and our dinner at night. She was excellent in teaching me how to care for myself, how to cook and clean and even sew clothes. I adored her so. It took about a year for me to recover after she passed away. She and my grandfather (Joseph Lee Washington), were still together when my father, Isha, Joey and myself went to live with them on Hillcrest Avenue, but she was soon separated, and later divorced, from my Grandfather, not long after our arrival into their lives. I am not sure if we contributed to that separation, or if it was inevitable.

As I have stated earlier, it is important to provide my own history to allow the reader the opportunity to know many of the dynamics of my experiences that worked together to bring Imani into my life.

My grandfather, who appeared to me as a tall large frame man who towered over us, was an abusive man coming in at night and whipping us for no apparent reason. I don't have many memories of him, since I was very young at the time, except the memory of him in the kitchen cooking apples and eating raw onions and of course, the whippings. I do believe children should be whipped from time to time, but never abused. After their separation, he disappeared from our lives. I never saw my grandmother with another man after she and my grandfather were no longer together. He went on and remarried and moved to Westfield, New Jersey.

From what I am told, he also beat my grandmother, regularly. When I finally saw him more than twenty years after he disappeared, we didn't have much to say. I felt much resentment for him because he had never visited us.

I attended Cook School, an elementary school on Leland Avenue, where my fondest memories were racing home everyday with Dennis Curry, Troy Nuttingham, Tony Harrison (now known as Anthony Abdus Salaam), and Jeffrey Petterson. We had two teams. We would race to a designated street pole that symbolized the ending point of the race.

Everyday one of us on our team would take off out of the school doors and run as fast as we could for about a half of a mile or more, to that street pole. Back then, children didn't need a whole lot of money to have fun. We were creative. We played "red light", "tag", "scatter", "hide and seek", and as we got older, "hide and go get it".

We took our lunch to school many days. It consisted

mostly of bologna or egg salad sandwiches. I really hated those egg salad sandwiches! Back then, children didn't have access to refrigerators during school so you would put your lunch in the coatroom. By the time lunch hour came around that one egg salad sandwich would have the whole coatroom lit up with a powerful odor. After that, I remember throwing my egg salad sandwiches in the bushes everyday before I got to school to avoid the embarrassment and the taste.

I would stop at the gas station and use my milk money to get a candy bar. That lasted until the gas station owner told my father about my morning activities. You see, back then everybody knew everybody, and adults were not intimidated about helping another parent discipline their children.

It was usually on Christmas and birthdays that we would get invited to go to my mother's house. Spending the night there was a big event for Isha, Joey and myself. That is where we would get to stay up late and play with Michael and Mary Leigh. During the summers, she would sometimes come and pick us up and take us all to the beach at Sandy Hook, or to Greenbrook Park for a cookout. There is where we would play with our "make believe cousins", the Nicholsons, which consisted of the mother Redell and her children, Elijah, BarbaraAnn (which we pronounced Bar-Bran), Tracy, Theresa and Lori. Jeff Walker who was Ruby's son was also one of our make believe cousins. It may not seem like much, but those are the memories that you tend to cherish later in life. Redell and Ruby are like sisters to my mother and like aunts to us. Sometimes their children would also spend the night at my mother's house so the parents could stay up late playing cards. I can remember when we would be playing in the bedroom at night instead of going to sleep, and how one of adults would take a shoe off and come up to the room and beat us.

It wasn't abusive, it was just to let us know that all of the adults were watching us and that's the way it supposed to be. Like the saying goes… "IT TAKES A VILLAGE TO RAISE A CHILD".

We also spent occasional days and weekends at my Aunt Ruth Motley's house. The visits were occasional because we were only permitted to go to Aunt Ruth's house when she and my father were not engaged in a dispute. After a dispute that was not settled, they would hold a grudge for months at a time. Sometimes the feuds would last for months or years at a time. This was my father's only sibling. From what I could tell, Aunt Ruth was a gentle woman with a good loving spirit. Now, her house was the place that I could count on getting a big, big hug, when we walked in. The only other woman I remember, who hugged me like that as a child was my Aunt Katey Woodson, who lived with my other Aunt Mary Jefferson. Aunt Ruth's house is where I would hear her singing spiritual songs like "Swing Low, Sweet Chariot", accompanied by someone playing the piano and someone else on the guitar. This was also the place where I would smell real home cooked food in the kitchen and sometimes the terrible smell of "chitterlings". At the time, being so young I had no idea that they were the worst parts of the pig, but I did know that they carried an awful smell. That was the only bad thing that I can remember. Everything else was great!

We had so much fun, running around the house, with our cousins April and Paris, who were just a little older than we were. Their older brothers Buck, Reggie and Marion seemed at the time, much older than us, so we didn't play with them much. Their younger brother Darren, nicknamed "Wee Dee" was too young to keep up with us as we ran from room to room, jumping and playing. As we have gotten older, the age differences have had little relevance and we have been able to enjoy many good times at April's annual Fourth of July cook out and other family gatherings. April has now become the modern matriarch of the Washington and Motley families.

My oldest first cousin, Buck has always possessed what I call "quiet strength", and is a success story in himself. He has not only survived a coma, which the doctor's said he would never come out of, but has gone on to continue working on various computer projects and still comes out and video tapes many family events. His sister April, along with his wife Diana and others, was the main one who defied the doctor's predictions that he would never walk again, and instead went to the hospital everyday to talk to Buck until he eventually began to make progress. Reggie, who became one of my childhood heroes, seeing him engaged in the first "party brawl" I had ever seen, that featured him jumping on a car before leaping onto the person he was fighting. He later became a mentor to me as he inspired me to always be a businessman when I became an employee of his, in his janitorial business.

Marion was the good spirited brother who went off to the armed forces to serve his country and ended up as a computer technology wizard. It seemed like Marion always kept a big smile on his face and his smile was the type that became contagious. Even though Marion has passed on, I keep his picture on my bulletin board at work so whenever I need to be lifted up, I can look up and see his million-dollar smile! It seemed to me, that Paris and Wee Dee were the ones who developed a spirit similar to that of Aunt Ruth's, using the church as an integral part of raising their families.

This "village" concept is something that we, in the black communities in particular should strongly resurrect for our own survival. I say "in particular" because it is we who are so disconnected from our culture, morays and norms and have suffered the most because of that disconnection. Older folks and children should never fear going down to the local corner store. They should not be held hostage in their homes fearing that if they took an evening walk, that they would be in danger from some young "make believe" thug. As a "village" we should make sure everyone understands that the residents are protected and MUST BE RESPECTED by any means necessary.

The men in the community must monitor what goes on, at least on their own block. They should form coalitions with their neighbors and put some type of schedule together where they would know that someone in the coalition is watching out for things. When anyone violates the safety of our children, our women, our old folks, or anyone else for that matter, they should be dealt with accordingly. The only reason why most of the ills in the community plague us is because we allow them. ALWAYS REMEMBER THAT DARKNESS CAN ONLY EXIST WHEN THERE IS NO LIGHT.

# 3.
# THE NEIGHBORHOOD COMPONENT

***

Mid-way through fourth grade my household moved from the east to the west side of town. The household consisted of my grandmother, Mildred Washington, who had joined the ranks of single-motherhood with the separation from my grandfather a few years earlier, my father, Joseph Theodore Washington, my sister Isha, my brother Joey and myself. We moved on West 7th Street near Hobart Avenue, where Dwight and Mark Mitchell lived. They had moved to Plainfield from Newark. My brother and I would go and hang out with them at their home sometimes. Their family appeared to be very "wholesome" to me. They gave me that "something special" feeling because both the mother and father were present in the home and I noticed it, even at my young age. Their parents treated us nice, and their mother, in particular, kept them sharp by her regular church routine. Sometimes we would join them on Sunday and attend their church back in Newark. That was about the only time that we were ever in church as children and even those occurrences were few and far between.

My father or grandmother didn't include a church routine in their schedule and they never impressed it upon us. It was only a few times, on Easter, that my father attempted to persuade us to go down the street to the local church, which I was sure he had never visited. I was also pretty sure that he was more interested in the neighbors noticing that he had gotten us some new clothes, than he was with our spiritual advancement. I was young but pretty sharp in my thinking.

A little further up the road was Stelle Avenue. This is where I really grew up. Most of the guys like Curtis, Craig, Chucky, Joe and Gene, that I played football with in the street, lived on this block. Greg and Conway, who also lived in the area, sometimes joined us. Conway was my partner at times, especially when things got rough at home and I felt the need to run away, I would always go to Conway's house. The games started out as "touch" football but would sometimes get rough and almost turned into tackle when tempers would flare. These activities were normal for boys growing up. The white guys that played with us had initials for nicknames, like L.J. and T.J. Some days that we didn't play football we would play basketball. Some of the best games occurred when Chucky's cousins from Brooklyn would come over. Things would get very competitive then.

Other times we would all gather in the street to have elimination races. Dimp, Robin and Valerie, the girls who lived next door to Chucky, would join in for these activities. I couldn't run very fast, as a matter of fact, comparatively speaking, I was slow, so I didn't get involved to much with the racing. I was usually urged to race Robin, who was not only the girl they always tried to match me up with, but she was also about the fastest person on the block besides maybe Chucky. I would of course always turn down such challenges.

At night, if we had permission to stay out a little later, we would go to Chucky's house or next door to the girls house or just stay on the street and talk. If we didn't get permission, sometimes we stayed out anyway and would suffer some type of reciprocation from our father. Needless to say, the neighborhood guys and girls wouldn't see us around for a few weeks. Sometimes the girls would have house parties. Their parents were the liberal type but they were not pushovers. They would invite just about everyone in the neighborhood and some of their friends and cousins from Piscataway, a neighboring town, just a few miles away. We had many good times at these parties which always added an element of suspense trying to guess who would end up dancing together and liking each other after the party.

I never did end up with Robin as a girlfriend but one of her cousins, caught my eye at one of the parties. She was older than I was but I "upgraded" my age by a few years and we became friends. I knew it was wrong to lie about my age so I apologized for it later. These activities, mostly good, made for great summers.

A decent neighborhood is invaluable because it contributes to the development of the children who live there. Decent neighborhoods, in most cases produce respectable children who grow up with integrity and a sense of purpose. There are, of course, exceptions to this. When adults only go to work and come home and never intermingle with their neighborhood where their children go hang out and play, then they are basically disregarding much of what develops that child. It's like never visiting the school that your child attends. We should visit the schools to assist the teachers by reinforcing what the children are learning and also to provide constructive criticism that will enhance the overall school curriculum. Teachers work very hard and should be commended for their work but there are always a few bad apples in every bunch. So parents should visit the schools and the neighborhoods regularly. The neighborhood is also a "school" that can teach both good and evil. NEVER UNDERESTIMATE THE POWER OF THE NEIGHBORHOOD!

## 4.
## THE INNER SANCTUM

***

I don't recall going many places as a family, probably because we didn't. My father wasn't the type to take us to amusement parks or ball games or much of anything for that matter. We kept busy trying to keep up with the daily chores. Imagine trying to keep a house with more than twenty rooms, clean. Then imagine cleaning up after a German shepherd named Devil that sometimes stayed in the basement for a week before my father realized that my brother and I had gone on strike and didn't take her out to relieve herself. Cleaning up after that dog and doing the other regular chores was enough to basically keep us on "lockdown" in the house. I don't even remember going to the park with my father. Even when I played football in high school, he rarely came to a game. We had to improvise around the house, which often times led to something getting broken, which led to another whipping. My brother and I used broom sticks and rocks in place of baseball bats and balls. Real baseballs or basketballs would have seemed like luxuries back then in a household where money was always "tight". We grew up on Corn Flakes or Oatmeal for breakfast. If Captain Crunch made it into our house there was need for celebration. Those were the good old days!

After school we would come home and just make up a

snack to eat. It could be anything from fried bread to a syrup sandwich. For dinner we had things like spaghetti from the can, lima beans or split pea soup with spam. That's right spam! We were so poor we couldn't afford ham, so my father would get spam. It came in a can with some kind of key that was used to open it up. It's funny how you can always remember the nasty things. I used to sit at the table for hours at dinner time with a mouthful of food, refusing to chew or swallow. Many times I would fall asleep with my face falling into the plate of food in front of me. I'm sure my father told us the same thing that I tell my children today… "eat your food and remember that there are children in the world who have no food at all".

My father, like his father, was also a strict disciplinarian. He would whip us at the "drop of a dime". I remember being awakened in the middle of the night to get a whipping because someone did not take out the garbage. It didn't matter whose turn it was to do any particular chore, if it was not done, my brother and I would both be the victims of my father's wrath. He wasn't home many days when we got home from school and many days we would already be in bed before he got home. That left my grandmother to take on the disciplinarian role, which she was not exactly cut out for. We would run around and cause havoc, like most children do, and if my father called my grandmother to get a report on our behavior, we would have to deal with him when he got home.

We didn't just do the regular childhood chores. We went over and above the call of duty. I sometimes likened us to slaves on a plantation. We would not only sand, paint and knock down walls but we would also clean up dog mess regularly and rake and shovel our property which was about 70 feet wide and about 250 feet deep. The ultimate task we performed that I will never forget is when a water pipe burst and Melvin, my oldest brother, Joey and I dug a trench that was about 60 feet long and four feet deep in order for the pipe to be repaired. I guess my father didn't take great stock in contractor's. He did however contribute in a positive way to my adulthood by providing me with carpentry and cleaning skills, which I have utilized time and time again. I will always appreciate him for that. That appreciation allows me to move forward in life without holding any resentment for him at all. We don't currently engage in any communication at all but there is not any animosity within me.

One of the things however, that is most prominent is the memory of when I took my first born son to visit his great grandmother and hearing my father say that we should stop bringing our children around with those "African" names. He was referring to Isha's daughters, Ameerah and Jameela whose "Arabic" names he obviously had a hard time pronouncing. Now, with the arrival of my son with the name of Tariq, another "Arabic" name was just too much for him to bear.

My father hung out quite frequently, usually returning home with the all too familiar, alcohol breath. On occasion, he would take my brother Joe and I with him to adult spots like Abe's Disco Lounge in Newark, (which was known in later years as Club Zanzibar) or Rocco's in Plainfield.

Every now and then my father would have a friend or two over to the house to have some drinks. Walter Barnett, who was like family would come over, sometimes joined by his children David, Kiesha, Dina and Bernard. Jesse Marshall would also visit, joined by his nephew Troy who also became like family to us. We would also on occasion join my father when he visited their homes.

My grandmother's brother, Uncle Melvin, who is now deceased, lived with us many years and would always provide the best entertainment during these drinking occasions. He was my favorite uncle and when he got "twisted" he would stagger all around the house and sometimes he would even fall down the steps. In the morning, he felt no pain and would deny that it ever happened. He always treated me good, sharing freely his clothes and his money and I really miss him. We looked on at the gathering of men and listened from a nearby room. As the alcohol supply on the table got lower and lower, the conversations would get louder and louder. Sometimes heated arguments would break out. These are the images that I grew up with. In retrospect, it is no wonder that I began drinking alcohol regularly myself at the tender age of about twelve.

# 5.
# GROWING UP TOO FAST

***

My everyday drinking partners from Hubbard School were Marvin and Rasado. We all attended Hubbard School in the 6th, 7th and 8th grade. We took turns bringing some of our parent's alcohol to school in mayonnaise jars and other bottles and would take them into the bathroom and get "twisted". This was almost a daily occurrence until Mr. Dickey, the only security officer in the entire school happened to catch us one day. We all got kicked out of school compliments of Mr. Jingelespy, the Vice Principle, and upon our return, that activity ended. Being dubbed "the three wino's" by what appeared at that time to be about half of the population of the school, who seemed to be waiting for us as we all somehow, without planning, walked in the main entrance at the same time, didn't help our school images. I still felt that we were pretty good guys because we hadn't yet indulged in other things that some of our peers were already using like "weed" and "pills".

Marvin and I were also regular party partners, along with his cousin Huey, and before each party we would normally each have a quart of beer. We would go to any available house party in Plainfield. It didn't matter how far it was... we would get there. We would talk about what we would do at the party, practice our dance moves and after the party was over we would discuss our successes.

I don't remember discussing our failures so I guess we left those out of the conversations. Back then, after we got established, every party felt like a success.

My father actually started me out on the party scene. My sister Isha was two years ahead of me in school so when she went to high school, I was still in seventh grade. She began asking my father if she could go to the high school dances that were held in the cafeteria. My father established a rule of thumb for her and that was… "yes you can go, but you have to take your brothers along". In the beginning, being only in seventh grade, I hated the idea of being "forced" to go to some high school party, but after going to a few dances and at first becoming what was known as "a wall flower", I soon bloomed into a regular party animal. A wall flower is the type of person who goes to a party and goes to some spot in the room and is basically in that same spot for the duration of the party.

I "graduated" from the wall after I realized that it was the wall flowers who were getting teased and the ones that didn't have much fun. Besides that, I also had another reason. I began to love all the attention the girls would give us, especially after we began dancing to slow records too.

Back then, in the 70's, disc jockeys always mixed in slow records throughout the night. Marvin and I would find the smaller petite high school girls and slow dance with them. Their girlfriends would sometimes stand nearby saying how "cute" we looked dancing. They knew we were younger, but we didn't care, especially since they thought we were so cute. We didn't even care that the girls obviously felt our "nature" rising as we danced close, sometimes "grinding", as we lacked the mental discipline to keep ourselves under control. We were young and didn't care. We knew we would get over any embarrassment we felt. After the slow dance was over

Marvin and I would huddle together to laugh and share notes. Sometimes my sister would get approval to go to a party but once we all got up the street we would split up and go our separate ways.

Our plan would be to meet back up and walk into the house together so my father would not suspect anything. The plan would fail of course when one of us didn't make it back at the appointed time. Many times my father was hanging out too and didn't find out that our plan had failed. My grandmother, who seemed to never sleep and always heard us trying to creep up the squeaky stairs, only occasionally "ratted" us out.

We also, loved going to the "Neighborhood House" on West Fourth Street or the "Teen Center" on South Second Street, for their parties. Sometimes they would have "Battle of the DJ's" where two DJ's would set up in different rooms and see who could lure the most people into the room they were playing music in.

The battles were great and a DJ could boost his reputation by being victorious. After the party we would always stop at Johnny's Corner, a late night "greasy spoon" type place on the corner of West Third Street and Lee Place, where we could always get an order of fries or some barbecue chips to kill that beer breath before heading home. Man, those were the days! We used to have a ball.

Because DJ's mixed in slow records throughout the night, a guy who wasn't too shy could always pick out a girl to dance close to and Marvin and I were both considered "veterans" by this time. At least in our own thinking. I never really knew Marvin's whole "story" and why he had always been able to hang out and go to so many parties. I'm sure he didn't know my whole story either.

My girlfriend was Karen Nashe in 8th grade. After

school, we would go over my friend Steve's house with his girl. Steve's parents were never home so he would go into one room with his girlfriend and Karen and I would be in another room. This is where we tried to perfect the art of kissing. We would kiss for hours at a time, until our jaws became sore. This is also where I discovered that a guy would suffer terrible pains usually referred to as "blue balls", if the call of nature wasn't answered in situations like that. Karen never gave in to my requests to advance our "boyfriend and girlfriend status" to the next level. I guess it was a good thing because I would have had no idea what to do anyway. I believe my mother, who was friends with her mother, actually had something do with us getting together and secretly had bigger hopes or plans for us in the future.

We did go to the prom together but once we went to high school our communication for some reason did not continue. I guess we both got busy with other things and people.

Imani in the meantime was attending Maxon School on the east side of Plainfield, but in the ninth grade, we both would attend Plainfield High School. In high school, we ran in different circles and never communicated except giving an occasional greeting as we passed each other in the hallway. I don't believe we even had any classes together. She was usually seen with her high school sweetheart, Poochie.

I wasn't really a bad student in high school but I did have my moments of being mischievous. I remember when Mrs. Freeman asked me to carry some things to her car towards the end of one school year and I ended up joy riding around with her car. I didn't mean any real harm and I did put the car back where I found it. Mrs. Freeman, by the way was one of my favorite teachers. She was ranked right up there with Mrs. Taylor, another one of my all time favorites. This was most likely around the same time that some of the neighborhood guys and myself would "borrow" cars from some of the local residents after we were sure they were in their beds for the night.

We didn't really mean any harm to anyone and would only use the cars for joy riding purposes. We even put gas in the cars! Things are much different and much more dangerous these days.

I got high on marijuana, or "weed" as we said, almost daily in my first two years in high school but always managed to keep my grades up. I supported my smoking activities by buying more than I needed and selling the surplus. That way I always had money AND weed. On special occasions, I would also mix in some beer or wine. A "special occasion" was any day that I just felt like drinking.

I found in most cases that I could camouflage a "weed high" unless the smoke was absorbed into my clothes but the "alcohol high" was much harder to hide, especially if it included wine. The weed high would also cause me to think about things deeply, which may have contributed to why I still sometimes over analyze things even to this day. I always say when I reflect though, that high school was a breeze. The work was never a problem for me. I never had to study much for tests especially in English or math. One English teacher appeared to get upset because I was able to do so well on the tests he would give.

Gary Jones (who is now deceased – the victim of a vicious, all white mob, who beat him to death with baseball bats and never got convicted of a crime), and I, would play around many days in the back of the class, but I always "aced" the tests. I was doing my thing, in school, enjoying the company of my friends and associates, Conway, Chucky, Craig, Tuggy, Duffy

(Mufeed), Jeff (Samad), Gary, Greg, Troy, Jeff (J.J), Leviticus, Johnny, Kevin (Kev), Antoine, Mark and Dwight, Lynne, Iris, Stacey, Leslie, Dimp, Robin, Valerie and others.

My first real high school "girlfriend" Riva Carson, lived on the east side of Plainfield but didn't attend Plainfield High. I believe her family was from Trinidad. Her mother liked me, and her father hated me. I couldn't blame him.

Riva and I were both fifteen and had no idea what we were doing when we simultaneously broke our virginity. I remember going into a panic a short time later as we both thought she may have gotten pregnant. We really liked each other but only stayed together for a short time.

Now, my "first love" was a beautiful and quiet young lady named Janet Striker. Her family was from Barbados and I loved her accent. Her mother really loved me and her father really hated me. I couldn't blame him either. We made love every chance we got. (I guess it was called "making love" back then, I'm not really sure). Most of the time the guys just called it "getting some". Whatever it was… it was good! I loved everything about her. I even loved how she said my name "Omar". I was with Troy Mitchell at the intersection of the main hallways that we sometimes called "Broad and Market", when I first noticed her walking down the hall. She had that sexy librarian look and none of the other guys even noticed her. She wore large rimmed eyeglasses and could easily go unnoticed. I said to Troy that "behind those glasses there is a star". I was right. I realized at an early age that I really desired an appreciated affection from the opposite sex (maybe a bit too much). What I didn't realize is that it may have been due to a lack of nurturing from my grandmother and mother. Janet and I stayed close until I went off to college. I guess the distance was too much for us to sustain what we had at such young ages. I still think about her from time to time wondering how she is doing and hoping her life has been good.

## 6.
## CHOICES AND CHANGE

***

I didn't start getting to know my mother in a "real" way until I moved in with her at the age of 15 after getting to the point where I didn't want my father hitting me unjustifiably. The truth is that I didn't want him to hit me any more at all. My words to him before I left were, "If I stay here, somebody is going to get hurt". I was just starting to take an interest in Islam, and my father warned me not to bring any of that "muslim stuff" in his house. He had seen some magazine articles about Malcolm X and Muhammad Ali in my room, during one of his random drug searches. My father would sometimes conduct full scale searches of my room while I was at school, looking for some drugs that he was sure I was under the influence of. Some days upon my arrival to the house he would call me in a room a do a "eye" check and a "breath" check. He would tell me that he knew I was using "dope". I interpreted "dope" as saying that I was using some very hard drugs, which I was not.

The only thing I ever did was drink and smoke weed and the only thing I kept in the room was weed but I had the best hiding places, like the fireplace that was just for show and the ornamental ceiling light fixture. I believed that if you found *my* stash, you could easily join the FBI or the CIA! I guess everybody feels like that about their favorite hiding places, until they're discovered.

I would later find that my mother on the other hand didn't mind me studying Islam and she was active herself in the community, working in various programs at the Neighborhood House and CAP. As a matter of fact, the first time I was blessed to hear and see Minister Louis Farrakhan, was around 1978, due to my mother receiving an award at the same program that he spoke in, at Plainfield High School. Later that year is when I joined the Nation of Islam.

I was invited to the Temple meeting, held at the home of Minister Linward X (now known as Karriem Muhammad), by Leviticus Rudolph. Jeff Owens (now known as Samad) and I walked together and arrived at the house on time. I forgot, however, about the weapons search that all who attended the Temple must undergo, and just before the F.O.I. (Fruit of Islam) soldier performed his check, I remembered that I had about ½ ounce of marijuana in my pocket.

You see, back then, putting weed in my pocket before leaving the house was as natural as putting on my socks. I excused myself to go stash the weed in some bushes and returned shortly thereafter. That was one of the great turning points in my life. It may have saved my young life. I could have easily become another urban statistic. Minister Linward X began teaching on various subjects and about how the black man and woman are righteous by NATURE and that it was time to accept our own and return to our true selves, which is being a righteous Muslim. I think I sweat more that day than ever before. It was hot that day, but not that hot! I believe it was the guilt coming out of me. Guilt because of the way I was living. Guilt has a way of making us sweat. That day, I accepted Islam as being my own.

About two or three years later, while attending Kean College in Union, New Jersey, after reciting certain required lessons and the actual facts I received my X, which represents the unknown last name that our forefathers and mothers were stripped of, during slavery. By this time, I held certain positions in the Nation of Islam, like Lieutenant and Assistant Minister. I never sought out titles and I always thought that the best brother was the one that didn't care about big titles but instead just got the job done.

I counted myself amongst that type of brother, but due to a lack of manpower, those titles were presented to me and I, reluctantly, accepted. Between 1979 and 1982, I traveled up and down the northeast coast from Boston , Mass. to Richmond, VA, as security for Minister Louis Farrakhan at a time when the "Nation" was not so popular. I also was blessed to meet and listen to Minister Farrakhan when he visited Minister Karriem's home in Plainfield, during that time. I am forever indebted to Minister Karriem for allowing me, at such a critical time of my life, that type of exposure to such a divinely inspired man. Farrakhan, like his teacher, the Honorable Elijah Muhammad is worthy of respect and honor for all of their hard work and the accomplishments they have made in civilizing so many uncivilized people. If you love people (and Black people in particular) then you should respect men like this because of the enormous amount of people that they have been blessed to help save, regardless of whether you accept Elijah Muhammad as the Messenger of God or not. I credit those men with saving my life, because when you grow up in the inner city, in the ghettos, there are so many negative forces pulling against you, that if you make it out with your life, you are truly blessed. One statistic stated that you had a better chance surviving in the Vietnam War than you do in the ghetto's of America, if you are between certain ages.

## 7.
## MEETING IN ELEVATED PLACES

***

Imani and I both graduated in the year 1979. Now, twenty-two years out of high school, there we were, in this beautiful edifice known as NJPAC. Imani, as always, had her hair perfectly pulled to the back which complimented her beautiful brown complexion, her magnetic eyes, her fine nose and her small to medium sized lips. She was fine back in high school and she was fine now. Imani was wearing a tan, plaid business suit and I had on a black business suit, white shirt and tie. I approached her not knowing exactly what I might say, but I felt confident. I guess I figured that I had been promoting the City of Newark all morning and now I could promote myself a bit. Anyway, we began to talk.

We spoke a little about why we were both there and she shared that she had hopes of getting some business from companies who were open to "spiritual instruction" for their employees. Somehow, the conversation changed quickly to a more personal one. Imani began to explain to me the type of man she wanted and that she was tired of the one-dimensional relationships she had experienced in the past.

I listened very intently. We then went and rejoined our parties and ate lunch, sitting at separate tables. After we ate we got back together and picked up where we left off with our conversation.

I don't remember every detail of the conversation, but Imani asked me two questions that I will never forget. She first asked me … "How are you coming at me?" I responded without missing a beat… "I'm coming at you in 3D". 3D? she asked. I said "yes, spiritually, mentally and physically, and in that order". Her smile said she approved of my answer. We talked some more as we walked outside and just when I thought I was done with the tough questions, she asked me…… What do you want from me? I said, "I want to have intercourse with your spirit and your mind, but not physically…. not now". Again, Imani expressed her approval with my answer with a bright smile. I was in the process of ending a bad relationship and was abstaining from sexual contact at that time anyway, so saying that was from the heart and it came out of my mouth easily and honestly.

That conversation, that first day, was the beginning of a beautiful and loving friendship and relationship that will remain with me the rest of my life. We exchanged numbers and hugged and I went back to work.

I felt good about our talk but wondered why in all of the years that we knew of each other we never had a real conversation, as we did this day. Even at our high school reunion just two years before, we were cordial, but no real conversation occurred. I guess there is truly a time and a place for everything.

Over the next few weeks we talked, and talked, and talked some more on the telephone, late at night involving our spiritual thoughts, our past histories and our future aspirations. I told her I remembered her from back when we were very young. In particular, I remember a time that we were both at a carnival when we were very young. There was a catholic school across from where I lived on Emerson Avenue, named

Saint Bernard's. They would have carnival's from time to time and I would go with my brother and sister usually coming back home with only a bag full of goldfish that would remain alive for only about a week after the carnival. I told Imani that as I walked up the steps in the catholic school back then, she reached over and touched my butt. I told her she was with another girl and they were laughing. She thought I was joking and said she was shy back then and couldn't imagine doing that, but we had a lot of fun talking and laughing about it.

We began having telephone conversations that lasted for many hours at a time. The conversations always flowed naturally and we would usually continue talking, even on work nights, until a yawn would ease it's way out of my mouth. Imani would then say, "you better go to sleep, sweetie". I'm sure if I hadn't yawned, we would have put in another thirty minutes or so, on the telephone. I loved talking to Imani so it really didn't matter. I once pulled out a telephone bill that had the amount of time we talked on the phone. I read off "100 minutes", "200 minutes" and over "300 minutes!". It was a good thing I got a "Tie-Line" service installed on the phone which allowed me unlimited minutes to her area code for a set amount of money each month.

We decided to get together for the first time at a neutral place one weeknight. It's always better to meet in a neutral place the first time to ensure that there is no pressure or expectations. Both people can feel comfortable knowing that the space they are both in projects equality.

Imani mentioned to her sister, Nina that she was going to meet with someone but did not give any details. We met at a halfway point on Route 22, near Scotch Plains, at a pool hall. We played a few games of pool and talked some more.

We were still feeling each other out but the night was

special. We affirmed our attraction for each other and ended the night with a big hug and a few short kisses. I remember feeling excited as I drove home almost as if I had just completed a successful high school prom date.

# 8.
# THREE DIMENSIONAL BONDING

***

We got together another time on a Saturday when she wanted to take a leather coat she had gotten for her mother, back to New York to exchange it. She rode to Newark and picked me up and off we went. We had good conversation the whole way over and we arrived on Orchard Street near the store where she purchased the coat. She went to look for another coat to exchange but could not find her mother's size in the same style coat. She told the salesman she would prefer to get a refund rather then come back to New York another time. The salesman was suggesting that she come back and the size she needed would be available at that time. Imani kept her cool but I could hear the salesman resisting the idea of giving a cash refund. I interjected into the conversation, putting a little extra volume and bass in my voice, "Is there a problem? What's the problem?" The salesman soon decided he would give her the refund after hearing Imani's clear explanation of why he should and I guess my little two cents that I added, didn't hurt. We left the shop and I felt that we had just accomplished our first unified victory over a common opponent.... THE SALESMAN.

After our defeat of the coat salesman, we went to get what I learned was one of Imani's favorite treats... Krispy Creme Doughnuts! She raved about these doughnuts until we got to the store. I was clowning around when we went into the store, saying that Krispy Creme was a cult and the patrons were like dope users. I was scratching my arms as we stood in line and using my best whining "dope fiend voice", I began saying, "HURRY UP...HURRY UP... I NEED MY DOUGHNUTS!" Well, this seemed to be embarrassing Imani a little and after a few minutes she urged me to stop. I must say that my act was entertaining to some of the other patrons. This act also became "a regular" every time we visited a Krispy Creme Doughnut store.

After we safely tucked a few boxes of doughnuts in her car we went to B.B. Kings Entertainment Complex on 42nd Street for dinner. I had broiled salmon and Imani had a steak with a potato. I asked if she wanted wine and she said no. Neither of us drank alcohol and as a matter of fact, alcohol or drugs were never a part of anything that we shared. That night we shared our very deep spiritual beliefs with each other. Imani spoke about deities that were closely connected to God. I equated some of what she said to the twelve major scientists taught to me in the Nation of Islam.

She spoke about how a person can change their very physical make-up based on the spirit that is within their body. We also talked about reincarnation and life after death. I said that I did not believe in reincarnation but I believed that a person can live on through others if they carry with them, the spirit of the one who had passed on. We did agree that the spirit needed a vessel to be housed in order to be recognized. Imani however felt that the vessel did not necessarily have to be human in nature. She felt that any living matter could house the spirit. I believe she also said that if she came back, that she would like to come back as a BUTTERFLY! So, here we are, sitting in this restaurant having a spiritual conversation and both parties were equally interested. This was so different for me. This is what I had always yearned for – A GENUINELY SPIRITUAL WOMAN.

When we left the restaurant the temperature outside must have dropped another twenty degrees and it was very cold and windy. We had parked quite a few blocks from the restaurant, I guess because we didn't have any special destination. We just knew we were hungry and wanted something to eat. Imani loved good food and when it was time to eat, she wanted to eat! We snuggled closely as we quickly walked to the car.

When we got to her car, I opened her door so she could get in. I always opened the door for her. It didn't matter if it was my car door or hers, I didn't want her to touch it. She liked that treatment but sometimes she would forget and open the car door slightly, then she would catch herself and say, "oops, sorry", and she would then close the door and allow me time to walk around the car and open it. She said she wasn't used to that so it would take some time to adjust.

We began spending more time together when our schedules allowed and our conversations included attempts to define "us". We came up with what we called "a loving friendship". I began to visit her at her condominium and was so pleased to see that she kept her place immaculately clean. I wondered where her "junk" was. I remember opening her closet door and saying, "I bet I know where some junk is", only to open the door and find one of the neatest closets I have ever seen in my life.

Now, by this time intimacy had also become a part of the relationship. We talked about commitment. I told her that I would commit physically to her, and would not be involved with anyone else, but I could not commit to her spiritually and mentally until she quit smoking cigarettes.

I felt that if I was to commit totally at that point, then I might end up with a woman who smoked cigarettes. Instead I said I would work with her in order to help her quit. I had made an exception with regards to the cigarettes. Normally I would not deal with anyone who smoked cigarettes.

Committing physically was easy for me because when we began bonding, I was living a celibate lifestyle so physical intimacy was not so important and she had already captured enough of my spirit and my mind to keep me away from, or even desiring, another woman. We experimented with making love. I use the term "experimented" because as I have stated, the physical part was the least of concerns for both of us. When two people are deeply bonded spiritually and mentally then physical intimacy can only be deeply intense. We soon came into that realization. When Imani would ask me if I wanted her to fall in love with me I would always respond by saying "not yet". I had just recently gotten out of a bad, short term, relationship and was trying to cope with that. I was still "buying" a little time but I was definitely beginning to see us being together permanently, in the not too distant future. This could be a valuable lesson for women who think the best way to "hook a man is with sex. I must disagree and say, if you really want him "hooked" then capture his mind and soul first.

We attempted to reverse our behavior at times and go back to being close but with no physical intimacy. We tried this for a few weeks. IT DIDN'T WORK! We had crossed a bridge and could not go back. We were enjoying every aspect of each other and this was all a part of what made us what we had become... loving friends.

I also began communicating honestly with the mother of my two young children about my past shortcomings, which included not being honest about other women, who I gave my attention to while still trying to foster a relationship with her in the past. Many times it is the residue of guilt that is our greatest deterrent in fostering a healthy relationship. Yes, I had issues! Imani helped me understand my issues and how I bought my own issues into being.

Imani had also made an exception with me, stating that she always made it a point, not to deal with anyone with small children. Imani had no children of her own. I have two young children, Asia and Omar. My oldest son, Tariq was now nineteen living in Georgia and attending college and therefore was not an issue to be dealt with. Imani was concerned about my relationship with my children's mother.

I told her that I would always love my children's mother for giving birth to my children and for the many things she has done for me and that we had a good arrangement taking care of our children and she should not be concerned about that. Imani wanted assurance that there would be no interference in what we were building. She would say things like "it's all or nothing" to help me understand that it was a very serious issue.

On Valentine's Day Imani sent me one dozen yellow roses. I was indeed pleasantly surprised when they arrived at my job. I called Imani right away to thank her. The card that came with the flowers said, "For every loving year of friendship I will replace one yellow rose with a red one". We had a conversation not long before about the colors of roses and what they represented. Yellow representing friendship and red representing passion. I made an arrangement for Imani consisting of yellow and purple silk flowers. Purple, of course representing royalty.

I really enjoyed the fact that Imani and I always seemed to do things with a purpose and a meaning. Imani came to me at the right time in my life to help me with my issues. She made me understand that I drew most of the drama in my life, to myself, due to not being totally honest with others and myself.

We went out to dinner one night in New Brunswick, New Jersey one night to hear some music at a place called Makeda's. They had a live band and they also had a sectioned off area that had many different African and cultural items on display. We slowly milled around the area admiring the masks, clothing, incense, and other items they had on display. We felt, and I'm sure we looked to others, like we were a couple who had been together for a few years and were very pleased with each other. We just didn't appear to be two people who were together for only a few months. It was a natural and comfortable fit.

We sat down at a table and ordered some appetizers and Imani ordered some Egyptian tea. They served honey for the tea and she began pouring it in her cup. When I tasted it, I started looking for the pancakes. It was so SWEET! Imani liked her tea sweet. The band was playing and they sounded good. The atmosphere was great. We saw Lana Armstrong at a table nearby. Imani had good words to say about Lana, saying that she was a nice person. I agreed and said I remembered her as far back as elementary school. As Lana passed our table on her way out we kissed her and said goodbye. We were all in the class of 1979. Being from the class of Plainfield High School's class of 1979 just made you feel like family.

The music began to pick up so we moved closer to the band. We sat a while but the music got so good we found ourselves up dancing along with the music. We stayed until the band's set ended. On the way back to the car, we casually walked along the streets gazing up at the Crossroads and the State Theaters. She pointed out a business that a friend of hers had nearby. I felt fulfilled as we talked on our way back to her place. It was another wonderful night.

Sometimes we would get together and share a more peaceful day or evening. I would bring over something to cook like fresh salmon or some fresh vegetables and fruits. I showed Imani how to broil the salmon and I made a sauce with cranberries, butter and honey to glaze over the fish. I had never done it before but I wanted something special for us. I made some broccoli with cheese and Imani made some rice. It was a delicious meal. I sat down and Imani prepared the plates. She normally prepared the plates. Food always seems to taste better to me if a woman prepares the plate. Especially when the woman loves you. I am not being chauvinistic… it's just how I feel. Imani didn't cook much herself. She had not perfected this particular skill but what was important to me was that she didn't mind trying.

We sometimes laughed about the first meal she cooked for me that consisted of some over baked chicken wings and some soupy rice. I struggled through most of it but was inspired from that point on, to assist when I could, in the kitchen. We would talk over dinner or after dinner, sitting at the table or relaxing on the couch and we would share our histories with one another.

Some nights, we would also watch movies together, professional boxing, tapes of Minister Farrakhan, or Imani would share some of her reading material with me. I didn't read much myself but I would enjoy discussing the material she had pertaining mostly to spiritual subjects. She had all types of books and when something we would say sparked a thought relating to something she read, she would say, " I want to read something to you, do you want to hear it?" I would say "sure" and then take a deep breath, because I knew we where about to go on a spiritual and mental journey. It may have been about any number of different subjects including health, religion, integrity, relationships, character, or BETRAYAL.

Imani and I took the time to carefully listen to each other when one was speaking. I had read an email that had excerpts of a speech made by T.D. Jakes. One of the questions that he raised that was related to relationships was… Are you with the person you would want to be with and hold your hand if you got some terrible news like your mother just died? T.D. Jakes went on to say, that if you are not, then you need to re-examine your relationship because you may not be with the one you should be with. Now, I don't remember his exact words but the point he was making, struck a cord in me and I had to share that with Imani. Of course I had to ask her, who was the person she would want to be holding her hand if she received such news. I would not have wanted something like that to happen, but I am happy to say that she said I was that one.

## 9.
## THE NEIGHBORHOOD MOTHER

***

In my neighborhood, back when I was very young, the neighborhood mother was my friend Chucky's mom. She along with Chucky's grandmother took good care of us. She was just like a mother to me. She fed us and always gave us something cold to drink. We even shared time with his father, a former professional basketball player, who would give us pointers and show us some of his classic moves. They were a special couple and a good role model for us as children. It is so important for children to be exposed to positive images as they grow up. This will be of great consequence when they come to the crossroads of choosing between doing good or going down the wrong path. Good role models provide the notion that *"doing the right thing"* provides a good future and great benefits.

Parents should expose their children to the finer things in life to let them know that they are attainable, even if it means taking a ride every now and then to that "nice part of town". Sadly, too many children never escape the sights and sounds of the ghetto and never get a vision of the great things that they can accomplish.

A neighborhood mother allows you access to her home *and* her family because she accepts you as family also. From what I am told, Mrs. Cole was and is this type of person. If you wanted something to eat or drink as a child and you were on their block, then all you had to do was stop by the Cole's house and everything would be okay. THIS IS A WOMAN WHO INDEED MUST BE HONORED.

Mr. Cole should also be honored because someone has to finance the cost of being charitable. Mr. Cole was the type of man that would rather have too much food and drinks for guests rather then not enough. That sentiment was echoed years later from Vern McDuffie, another father figure to me. He too, would always make sure that there was an excess amount of food available at parties and cookouts.

The neighborhood mother concept is one that is so vitally important in today's society. This one role alone dispels any notion of a man being superior to a woman. No man can ever be the equivalent to the neighborhood mother, yet this role carries the answer to many of the ills that plague our communities. The universal ingredient that this "mother" offers is love. Love is what most of those young men lack, who are imprisoned right now in jails across the country. Love from a "mother" has enough power in it to block any superficial attraction that one of our youth may have for a "gang" or a drug or any other vice.

# 10.
# BETRAYAL

***

Imani had a real issue with betrayal explaining to me that in a past relationship she had went away on trip to Georgia and returned home early to only find her mate, who she was living with at the time, had another woman in her home and in her bed! She spent many years dealing with that and felt that whoever she was with in the future, must never, ever betray her. I am happy to say that once our commitment was stated, I never violated what I said. That's right! There was no double dipping when it came to Imani. It should never be any double dipping with anyone when you have a commitment. She bought and delivered that message to me. She had my full attention and she was my only interest, so it was easy.

Imani understood her God given right to choose. She knew that she could re-analyze her relationships at any given point and then make a conscious decision whether she would continue on the same way in that relationship or whether she would request that a change take place. She was strong enough to make a decision that was best for her spiritual and mental livelihood even though her emotions were "in the mix." That occurred once with us for a short time and we didn't contact each other for a few weeks but I sent her a poem entitled "Some Kinda Special" and that initiated our communication once again.

Many women, and also some men, do not understand that

they have this choice and feel they are *stuck* in their relationship even though they feel it is going nowhere. Such an imbalance in emotions allows for physical or mental abuse to sometimes set in. That abuse can come from the other person in the relationship or in can be self-inflicted. To avoid abuse, say what you mean and mean what you say. If you want to be married and the person you are with does not want to be, then you should choose to change your situation. It's as simple as that.

## 11.
## HISTORY AND UNIVERSAL LAWS

***

One night we decided to do something a little different. It was during the week but I always tried to take advantage of some of the events going on during "Black History Month". This particular night, Paul Robeson Jr. was speaking at a nearby college. I believe it was Rutgers. We went to the event that was filled with a mostly white audience. He showed a short video of his father, Paul Robeson and his accomplishments. Imani and I were armed with yogurt covered pretzels and raisins. We had a light dinner before we left consisting only of some yellow and green squash with onions and some corn on the cob. After the video Paul Robeson Jr. spoke. We were both impressed with what he had to say. I began calling him "the sneaky radical". We had a good laugh about it later. He was very enlightening and we both enjoyed what we heard.

Imani really admired Harriet Tubman. She said Ms. Tubman was her hero. I went to a play one day and took my children with me. Imani wanted to go but she had something else on her schedule and I wasn't exactly sure if it was a play about Harriet Tubman or someone else. I had called the theatre in the city of Rahway the day before to check and they actually told me that the play was about Rosa Parks. I believe Imani had gone to get a facial that afternoon. She got her facial done regularly. She was a little disappointed later when I told her it was indeed a play about Harriet Tubman.

Imani began teaching me about the different chakras throughout the body and the effects they have on our emotions and our physical and mental health. She asked me to lay on the floor one day so she could guide me into the understanding of chakras. I was suffering with some pain in my back. She was working on me as she tried to dissect my deepest feelings, stating that our physical pain is sometimes a result of our mental and emotional state. She read excerpts of a book that dealt with the chakra points on our bodies. As she instructed me, I always felt a great sense of admiration because I knew she wasn't wasting time. I knew that she was genuinely dedicated to the knowledge she had acquired and I appreciated the fact that she was willing to share it with me.

Imani gave me *three* sheets of paper one day with information on it from some of her studies, some of it dealing with chakras and other parts that discussed harmony and universal laws. She told me that it was my chart, (or at least a part of it). One page dealt with the fifth chakra which was identified as the "throat" chakra. This was the area that dealt with communication and telling the "microscopic" truth. She wrote that I should wear the color blue as much as I can. These words of course jumped right out at me because I learned in the Nation that "blue" is the color of deceit, since the sky and the sea both look blue but in reality neither is the case. Even still, we as F.O.I. wore "blue" uniforms BUT with the symbol of freedom, justice and equality on our shoulders. These two items, telling the truth and wearing blue, were both connected to the mental plane. This same page also discussed "Age Chronology" which was connected to the emotional plane. She wrote that it was something that occurred in my life between the ages of twenty-one and twenty-eight that had a profound impact on me. She wrote that I should try and remember what I experienced during that time period that I had never forgiven. She wrote that I needed to forgive whatever happened so that I would be able allow something "new" to come into my being.

Another page included information concerning some of the natural laws and were documented as follows:

*The Law of Creation* – All things invisible, formless, non-manifested, are made manifest into a visible form as the mind acts upon substance

*The Law of Compensation* – The law of substance that equalizes all things. To realize and maintain Divine Order, substance must have both an inlet and an outlet in consciousness and must keep moving. To demonstrate substance as supply, the law governing it must be recognized and kept. Those who, due to pride or ignorance, do not open themselves to the inflow of substance, do not demonstrate supply, and all who by selfishness refuse an outlet, also fail. Everyone must receive freely and give freely as they receive. Disregard of the basic principle of supply frequently hinders man's realization of the Divine good. Readiness to give and readiness to receive are equally essential.

*The Law of Correspondents* – The subjective world contains an image of everything which is reflected in the objective world.

*How we create:*

1. Consciously by choice
2. Unconsciously by thought, word, deed, feelings or secret thoughts
3. By default – by not choosing

***

One of the pages dealt solely with "HARMONY" and read:

*Divine Harmony* – Perfect accord with the goodness, the beauty and the righteousness of the Omnipresent Spirit. Everything is governed by fixed law and harmony is it's expression. This is illustrated by the living body, which is a sensitive instrument, responsive to the touch of the master (I AM).

*Divine Harmony (How it is Lost)* – When the will is centered in the external and loses sight of the ideal, it breaks the connection between spirit and manifestation, and thus man loses the harmony that is under Divine Law.

*Divine Harmony (How it is Restored)* – Through a knowledge of the "Truth of Being", man is restored to Divine harmony. He must know the truth about himself and conform to it in all his thinking and not be misled by appearances.

Imani, also articulated this information that was given to me in writing. She also provided the right spirit in relaying this new and somewhat strange information. I didn't understand it all then and I'm sure the more I read it, the more I will get out of it. I just felt blessed to have someone who cared enough to provide information to me that would make me a better person. Being able to articulate this type of information, I'm sure is what contributed to me asking Imani to do a taping of herself speaking which could be marketed in various magazines. She initially shrugged off the idea, but being the business type that I am, I realized that she had a marketable gift that others could benefit from, so I didn't let the idea rest.

I told her I would handle all of the production and promotion costs of the project and the proceeds would go towards the spiritual center that she wanted to build. She liked the idea but she still felt she wasn't quite ready. This is one of the reasons why I know we were meant to merge paths. I was made ready, through my own past experiences, to recognize her gifts and assist her in such a way that would allow others, who would otherwise never be exposed to what she had to offer, to benefit from her mind and spirit.

# 12.
# SHE SPOKE TO THE WORLD

***

I called Imani on February 26, 2002 (remember these two numbers, the two and the six) and asked her to meet me in the park with some of her lessons. I asked her what she was wearing and I asked her to wear something nice. She agreed. It was a Tuesday but I had taken off from work as I always do on February 26th in celebration of Master Fard Muhammad's birthday. This day is referred to as "Saviour's Day" by the Muslims. The book "Our Saviour Has Arrived", by Elijah Muhammad, will provide the reader with a deeper understanding on this subject. I told Imani that I had planned to go to Plainfield that evening to my friend Edward Anderson's mother's wake.

Edward (also known as Jockey and Zaid) and I grew up about two houses from each other on West Fourth Street. He knows my family better than I know his, because it wasn't until I was in tenth grade that I moved there on Fourth Street with my mother.

I have a great respect for Edward because of his accomplishments he has made in his life. At a young age he mastered the martial arts which allowed him to travel to other countries. He later trained other young soldiers and me when he became a member of the F.O.I., the military arm of the Nation of Islam. We would all jog down to Greenbrook

Park where we would work out, read and meditate by the stream. He has made tremendous strides and has gained many certifications in the field of computer technology. He has also taken on probably the greatest role ever, that being a family man. He along with my other friends, Greg and his wife Sandy, have provided priceless positive images for those aspiring to have successful marriages, especially those of us who have tried it but can't seem to quite get it right. They probably don't even realize the great impact that they have not only on their friends like me but also on their families. Greg and Sandy have taken things even a step further by staying active with the community, assisting with youth events, coaching and planning class reunion events.

Before his mother's wake, I met with Imani in the park and she began to speak in a very comfortable and natural way to the video camera that I bought along. She thought she wasn't quite ready for this taping but I knew that she was. When we discussed making a tape of her giving spiritual lessons, she would say she needed about six months to prepare. I guess she didn't always realize how God had prepared her. Once she began, she spoke as if she was talking to the whole world. In retrospect, I guess she was.

The following excerpts are from that meeting in the park:

***

*Speaking: Imani Amour on February 26, 2002*
*Opening Prayer:*

**Dear Father, Mother, Spirit God, Higher Self, Divine Self, Guardian Angels, Ancestors and God, I am now open to your guidance and support. I ask you Holy Spirit, to come down, come through me and deliver to the earth plane, the messages that you want us to learn.**

***

*Her Opening*

I am going to talk about spirituality. I want to talk to you about life, I want to talk about my life's purpose and hope that, it would help someone else realize what their life purpose is. I want to talk about love, I want to talk about relationships.

***

*On the purpose of life:*

I believe in my soul the reason that we are here on this earth plane and our life's purpose collectively is to love. Each and every one of us has within that realm an individual purpose. My life purpose is to bring joy and unconditional love to the world, and I'll talk about how I came to that conclusion. Over the years I have done a lot of spiritual work and used different techniques to clean up my vessel. What you see here before you today, I believe is the body that houses the spirit.

***

*On Relationships:*

Relationships are about how we love one another. Relationships are about how honest we are with one another. Relationships are about how we respect one another and relationships are about how we trust one another. The ultimate relationship is the relationship with God. And God is love, God is truth and God is trust. God is all honoring and when in a relationship, whether it be with your mother, your father, your husband, your wife, your children, if it's not representing God qualities, it's not of God.

***

*On the Kingdom of God:*

God says, and I believe, that the Kingdom is available to us if you practice the principals and the laws. The Kingdom is available, but when you choose to stay in a relationship that no longer serves your highest greatest good, and when you choose to stay in habitual behavior and choose to stay in a relationship that is toxic and that is no good for either participant, then you are not worshiping and honoring God's laws and principals. I believe the first relationship that has to be and must be in order is our relationship with God.

***

*On making a stand:*

Standing up for who you are, honoring yourself, honoring the God within you, honoring the other participant, seeing the loving essence of the other participant, knowing that God is there, regardless to what it looks like. We have to know that when our world is turned upside down, when we are experiencing something less than harmony, we are out of order with one of the laws or we are out of order with some of the principals. God will get you to move to your highest greatest goods even when you don't want to. So you can hold on, you can scream, you can shout, but if it's not God's will, it's not going to work.

*On starting her journey:*

I began my journey approximately twelve or thirteen years ago and I believe what brought me to this experience was a calling. Growing up my parents never instilled any particular religion within me, but what they did instill in me, was God. Then I had another traumatic experience that took me away from God and I spent many, many,

many, years in search of what was the purpose, what was the purpose to this whole thing they call life.

***

*On being a Spiritualist:*

As a spiritualist, as a practicing spiritualist, I have allowed myself, my heart to be open, I have allowed God to come through me to use me, to use my body as a vessel of life to help the planet heal. I've worked with many traditions. I've worked with many different men and women who were also discovering their spiritual gifts who were my teachers, who had different techniques and different models of healing. I've worked with RaKey Masters, I've worked with Listening Masters, I've worked with various priest and priestesses from different traditions and it all was not an easy ride. I'm sure as you probably feeling right now possibly a little uncomfortable, when these ideas and these models were first presented to me, I was also uncomfortable.

If I have learned anything through my experience and from my journey, it's that it's okay to be open, it's okay to be willing, it's okay to learn something new. If you feel as though that this is something, that you might be interested in, then I suggest you open your heart, make a commitment to get to know yourself and to get to know God and meet as many masters as you possibly can and open your consciousness to the many, many traditions of living, learning, loving and just being your honest, greatest self.

***

*This lesson is from November 7, 2001*

I was working by myself because it seemed like I wasn't living my fullest potential. I was reading this

book at the time, and the title of that book was, "I Will Not Die an Unlived Life" and the question that I had to answer was, "What are the courageous conversations I need to have with myself? The answer to that question seemed to flow out of me easily, effortlessly and joyously as if something was doing the work for me.
This is the answer to the question that seemed to flow through me effortlessly; It is fall and a time for all the old to go to the position of dying to make room for the possibility of what would be next. To be courageous and converse with myself about what fear has caused me to live an unlived life. Which has caused my heart to block itself and shut down from the full possibility and potential of loving unconditionally, fearlessly and fiercely. Years ago I lived that way, I'm going to say at times consciously and at times unconsciously in a drunken stupor for life. Part of that haunts me today and has robbed me of my full potential of love and loving. That was yesterday, but today I say no more, it is time to say goodbye, to unlock the door and to push the gate open to my self-imposed jail.

***

*More on Relationships*

Relationships are, in my opinion the basis for us being here. Whether it be a relationship with God, our relationship with our parents, our relationship with our siblings, our relationship with our children, our relationship with our friends, our extended family. I think relationships today, are not operating at there fullest potential.

I believe the reason why relationships are not operating at their fullest potential is because a lot of us have lost the most important connection that there is and that connection is our connection to God. Relationships are God's gift to us. Relationships come into our life to teach us more about ourselves and more our shortcomings, our fears, our guilt's, our shame, our pain. The one thing I want to emphasize about relationships is - when you get to know God, and that's the ultimate relationship, until we are willing to say, no, when things don't feel right, when things don't feel good, and until we are willing to walk away with everything or nothing, our relationship with God is not at a maximum possibility. God is love, God is light, God is all we need and I know today that I see God in each and everyone of you.

I know today that I am as God created me and I know today my relationship with God is not about going half way, it's about being willing to walk away with everything or nothing.

To the human family; the way that we are going to save ourselves, from ourselves, is to get back to God.... wholly back to God.

***

*Spiritual Prosperity and Healing Principal #1 Truth:*

Now I would like to share with you, some basic things that you can do start on your Spiritual Prosperity and Spiritual Healing. The first thing, tell the truth, tell the truth to yourself about where you are in life, whether you're hiding, whether you're in fear, whether you're in guilt, or experiencing shame, tell the truth. Stand up and tell the truth. Write it down and tell somebody exactly what's on your heart. It doesn't matter how ugly it is, it doesn't matter how shameful it is, I don't care what it is, because God has unlimited grace and mercy. The first

Principal towards Spiritual Healing and Enlightenment is to tell the truth, the absolute microscopic truth, tell it.

***

*Spiritual Prosperity and Healing Principal #2 Forgive:*

The second principle for Spiritual prosperity and healing is Forgiveness. You must, you have too forgive yourself and each and every individual who you hold in judgment, who you feel as though violated you, committed some type of atrocious act against you, shamed you, hurt you, you have to be willing to forgive at the deepest level of your being.

When we forgive, we are not doing it for the other person, were doing it for ourselves as a means of cleaning up and out our vessels, because when you forgive you are forgiving of something so something can come in anew, so forgiveness is absolutely important. Take a piece of paper and write it twenty-five times for each person; I forgive this person because... I forgive this person because… and keep doing it until nothing else comes up to you and if you have to do it daily, hourly, by the minute or by the second, do it! The forgiveness that you offer up to the universe will be taken away from your being and then your universe will be able to bring something anew to your being.

***

*Spiritual Prosperity and Healing Principal #3 Trust:*

You must learn to trust God. You must learn to trust that God is always operating in us, as us and through us. You must learn to trust yourself. You must learn that when the Spiritual Being learns to trust, that's when we make our connection, our highest connection with God. When we trust enough to know that we are being guided

**and directed to our highest greatest good. Trust that you know, trust your intuition. When you are in fear and for some reason you can't muster up the trust, do it anyway, do it anyway! That's your connection to God! That's your connection to Angels!**

I like to support the universe because I really do trust that all of us, all of you that I see, is God. So put your trust cap on and learn how to really trust, absolutely trust God, absolutely trust yourself, absolutely trust your brothers and sisters, because God is in all that exist.

## 13.
## IT'S ALL OR NOTHING

***

After Imani finished speaking to what seemed like the entire world, I kept the camera running and invited her back in front of the camera once again. This time she began speaking to me specifically and directly. The words spoken by her on that day, challenged me and caused me to question my own intentions and integrity. The conversation proceeded as follows:

***

*Imani*: **Sweetie…. One day….one day. Do you know what I'm talking about? I want to talk about risks and relationships and co-commitments. I came across something in my reading today that said in a co-committed relationship, you must be willing to risk it all. To walk away with everything or walk away with nothing.**

**I am standing here today and I'm asking you…. What are you willing to risk? It's all or nothing.**

***

*My response*: My life

*Imani:* **I want it all or I walk away with nothing**

***

*My response*: What are we talking about? (Guys usually get stupid when they feel cornered. Even though there may not be any devious thoughts in our mind and even if we are not trying to play on both sides of the fence, there's something about our self- preservation that's one of the things that makes us different than a women.)

***

*Imani:* **We're talking about relationships. We're talking about a commitment. I'M TALKING ABOUT US! I'm just greedy! I want it all! Not half. Not a piece!**

**I think you're a little bit in fear. I think you are not so sure about moving on even though you have the real deal before you.**

***

*My Response:* Are you the real deal *for me?*

*Imani:* **Yes, I'm the real deal for you, if your willing to open your heart and if your willing to move forward and if your willing to stop making excuses. Be bold… Step into your bigness. Make a commitment to step into your bigness.**

**Forgive yourself for whatever judgements you hold against yourself.**

**Don't be held hostage to your past. If you want to go on with your future, then go.**

***

Imani began to admonish me regarding my not telling my children's mother about her and that we were involved in a relationship. I stated that I did not feel it was necessary at that time because she was still having a difficult time moving on with her own life, and even though we were no longer together, I did not want to put something on her that she could not handle. Imani responded by asking me:

**Do you think the truth is cold and unloving?**

***

I responded saying… **the truth is not but…..**

***

Imani: **This must be love because it freezing out here!**

Imani was referring to us being out in this increasingly chilly weather in February, in the park, having this discussion. I agreed and we decided to pack up and leave the park. I never finished my thought about truth not being cold. TRUTH IS NOT COLD, BUT THE METHOD IN WHICH WE PROVIDE TRUTH CAN BE VERY COLD!

Imani was very serious on this particular day and wanted me to understand that she was willing and able to make a well thought out decision regarding our future, if there was to be one. This of course depended on how I could handle the questions that she asked me. What I appreciated the most was the loving and tender way that she expressed her concerns and addressed her questions. It was always with the highest self-respect and self-honor. That of course is the prerequisite for respecting others. This method of communicating on such a high spiritual level, it seemed, she had just about perfected. I chronicled our very personal conversation to provide an example of conducting a very civilized conversation even though the topic was very sensitive.

I will venture to say that women, more often than not, do not engage in this type of conversation even though it is warranted. In most cases, they approach the conversation with anger, hostility and frustration or they avoid the talk altogether. Guys are even less likely to initiate a conversation like this at all. Imani believed in laying the facts out on the table and making CHOICES.

## 14.
## THE DIRECT CONNECTION

***

There is much that can be learned when studying a person who knows how to properly communicate with another. When two people speak to each other in this respectable manner it keeps the relationship on a very high level. A man's ego is not made to accept a woman talking down to him or calling him out of his name. Of course some men are more patient than others are. A woman's ego tends to not always be as fragile as men, but of course a woman should never be talked down to either. Low self-esteem may in some cases cause a woman to lash out in desperation. Hearing Imani speak in such a majestic manner was like a breath of fresh air. She had something in her that you can't get from mother or father or sister or brother. When she spoke you knew she had the spirit of God.

I believe that an Angel is one who has a direct connection with God. I believe that as an Angel, there is a certain mission that must be fulfilled and that there are particular things that an Angel must carry out while they are amongst us. The key element here is the direct connection with God. Imani believed that she had achieved that connection and her faith indeed made it a reality. Anyone, who truly knows the power of faith, can understand what I am saying. Imani acknowledged her past and present teachers and desired to continue receiving the tools that would sharpen her skills, but felt that she had grown to the point of not needing an intercessor when it came to communicating with God. This is why she wasn't thrilled with the "church routine" and the notion of going through a minister or anyone else as an intermediary in order to get a connection with God. We performed salat (prayer) together and meditated together but more importantly I saw how she was dedicated to her own spiritual development on a daily basis and I saw her actively sharing what she acquired, with others. You can never convince me that you have God, if you don't give charity to others.

Giving five dollars at the mosque or church is fine, but buying a sandwich for about five dollars and giving it to someone who is truly hungry, (not someone who is asking for money so they can go get high), and watching the joy on their face as they eat it is true and pure charity from the heart. Providing knowledge and wisdom is an even better method of providing charity. As they say, "it is better to teach a man to fish rather than buy him a fish". Imani was always willing to provide knowledge, wisdom, and understanding, and all with the spirit of God and this is why I truly believe that she attained that role of Angel.

# 15.
# A LOVELY EXCURSION

***

Imani would sometimes make the comment "I need to get away" which I initially interpreted as she was going away for a while and I would see her when she returned. I later found out that it meant in most cases that it would be nice if "we" went away somewhere. We began looking up different weekend and four or five day trips to places like Puerto Rico, Mexico, St. Thomas, and others. We figured that we would do a trip like that sometime in the summer of 2002. Another time we talked and she said, "I need to get to some sand and water". I told her if that's what she wanted, then that is what she should do. We agreed that we would both get some things done early the next day and then head down the Parkway to the shore. That's exactly what we did. We had no specific destination but we were together and we were happy. We looked at some information that I had gathered from the Internet that morning as we rode along, describing various bed and breakfast type places. We stopped at many different places in the Point Pleasant area but the prices seemed very high for what they were offering and we agreed to keep riding.

We made it all the way to Seaside Heights but didn't find anything that suited our tastes. One place even had a miniature movie theatre on the first level and plenty of goodies that we feasted on while we waited for someone to show us around, but the rooms were less than desirable. We had not eaten and by this time it was getting late and we were both very hungry. After all of that searching we decided to head back up north to find a more reasonable place and to get a good meal. Imani was pleased because before we left, we stopped so she could gaze at the water and the sand, which she said, was really all she wanted. How many couples can go on an excursion for one day and be loving and peaceful the whole day? In my experience, not many could survive the trip without some form of aggravation being manifested. Normally couples cannot agree on when and where they will eat. They may get frustrated with their plans not going exactly as they had planned. This was not a problem for us. We kept an even flow throughout the day, which reinforced the feeling that peace is indeed possible.

On our way back up north, Imani was on her cell phone talking to a friend of hers. I wasn't being nosey but I could not help over hearing some of the conversation. Imani listened very intently and asked many questions to the person on the telephone trying to ascertain the full story. Many times, we tend to not listen very closely to our family and friends and as a result we get only half of what they are actually trying to say. In some cases we train ourselves to only hear the negative side. In those same cases the positive side can out-weigh the negative but because of our impatience in our hearing, we miss the part of the conversation that would ease our temperaments. I have had conversations in the past that turned out bad only because neither I nor the person I was talking "at" had the patience to hear the whole story. Later, we would find out that what we thought was being said, wasn't really a true depiction of what was attempting to be relayed. Imani never displayed any type of confusion such as this. She was careful and wanted to collect all of the data surrounding what was being said to her so that she would be fully equipped to make a determination, if she chose to do so. I found this skill of hers to be compelling and rare.

As she began to explain to her friend all of the steps they needed to follow in order to regain control of a situation that had obviously gotten out of control, I realized that there were people who really depended on her counseling. I knew that I must have understanding and patience in a situation like this. Many times when people are on a "date", they try to monopolize the other person's freedom and time by becoming overbearing. Some people would never want to be in a situation where they are not the object of attention, 100% of the time. We must realize that sometimes we are *not* the most important issue, at all times. We must realize that our duty to help someone keep their sanity or just keep a cool head, takes precedence over our somewhat selfish desires. Of course this does not apply to other situations that do not require immediate attention or when two people should be spending quality time together, but one person decides to glue themselves into the television or engage in a meaningless conversation on the telephone. Now, that can be considered downright rude. Imani also explained to the person on the phone, all of the things that they should have done in order to avoid situations like the one they were in. She was honest but not overbearing. She was honest but she did not badger this friend of hers who was reaching out for assistance and understanding.

Sometimes people reach out for us because they believe we possess the knowledge and fortitude to explain, to teach, and to guide them and instead of providing these things, we give them the "cold shoulder". Whatever we are blessed to know, whether it is technical in nature or common sense, we have a duty to share it with others, especially when they come directly to us for assistance. Imani patiently walked her friend through the problem and took him to a safe mental place.

The next morning we went to breakfast at a place called "Le Peep" which was not to far from Imani's home. She had never been there and neither had I, so that already made it special. I never liked going somewhere with someone special, that they have been before with someone else or that I have previously been with someone else, because it tends to take away from the novelty of it all. Imani ordered some eggs and pancakes and I ordered a waffle with strawberries. We saw Lana Armstrong's brother with his family seated not far from our table. We had such a good time at breakfast. I remember Imani was trying to get me to stop taking all of the jelly packets from the table dispenser. I was casually putting them in my coat pocket for use at a later time.

We laughed and I, of course, kept shoving them in my pocket until the dispenser was empty. Our food arrived and we ate, sharing what we had with each other. The pancakes Imani had were huge and she could not finish them, so she had them wrapped and off we went.

I didn't stay once we got to Imani's house even though I wanted to. I always wanted to stay longer. It was Sunday and I had to pick up my children. I always make sure I spend time with my children. No one has to make me do that. I want to do it. Children are the greatest gift to us as parents. I am forever grateful to the mother of my children for bearing them with such pain and caring for them with love. She is a good woman who over the years that we spent together always tried to do her very best for me. I, in turn always tried to do my very best for her, supporting her and my children. It was the spiritual element that was the missing ingredient that my soul really yearned for, which did not allow our relationship to advance. I did not allow her to go back to work for the first six months of our children's lives even though I had to pay some of her bills, it was worth it since she was breast feeding the children and bonding during that time. As a matter of fact, she continued to breast feed them for their first two years.

I respect her for the sacrifices that she has made and putting up with me during the years we were together and for the care that she has given to my children. I don't understand it when adults don't take care of their children. I could never respect anyone who did not take care of his or her children.

So I left Imani's house to get my children, but the thoughts of this lovely excursion would resonate in my mind the rest of the day.

# 16.
# PURE ENJOYMENT

***

It's now the end of March 2002, and Imani and I are doing fine. We got together on a Saturday around 5:30 PM. When I got to Imani's house, she came outside with tennis rackets in her hand. She was ready to play and I joined right in with the same enthusiasm. It was still light enough out and a little chilly. We began walking to the tennis court passing by our classmate Mike Curry's condo, which wasn't far from hers. We saw Tony Davis and waved to him as we passed by. We got in just a few sets but the darkness quickly overtook the court and we had to postpone our tennis challenge until another time.

When we got back we continued with a conversation we had started earlier. We were trying to decide whether we would attend a party given by Benny Bell, another classmate of ours, who was about to relocate to North Carolina. Actually, this relocation had been going on for at least the last six months. We were in such good spirits after playing tennis and just being together, so we decided we would go to the party even though we had to pay to attend.

We had both thought that if your going to give a party, and dub it "A Going Away Party", then the host should pick up the tab. I said to Imani that Benny had recently rented space from me at my building in Newark, and we grew closer during that time, so I will support his venture. Imani liked Benny and also really wanted to see Aaron at the party and she wanted me to meet him. Aaron was a friend of hers who was also a friend of Benny's. So, we overlooked our judgements of poor taste and went to the party (again, Imani always told me to tell the "microscopic" truth). Benny explained later to me that he had nothing to do with the planning of the party.

It wouldn't have mattered where we went that night, we would have had a ball, and we did. We were both in the mood to dance that night. When we got there, we greeted some of the people we knew. It gave me a chance to see Benny's sister Hassana, who I always felt a special bond with. We both sort of grew up in the Nation of Islam, joining while we were still in our teens. Her husband Chris who I remembered from New York, and their sons were also there.

A short while later we were on the dance floor, having a great time. We danced and danced that night. I think I even danced more than Imani because I stayed on the floor doing all the "slide" dances too. I was having so much fun, I decided to get my small video camera from the car and capture some of the action on tape. I am glad I did because upon my return, Imani had Kevin Turner, another of our classmates, "voguing" while they were still sitting in their chairs. They were cracking up and having a ball.

The party ended but we were in no hurry to leave. Imani did a mini-fashion show for me in the hallway and then we sat around and talked for about twenty minutes. When I think about that night, I have to smile because we had so much fun!

## 17.
## THE DREAM AND THE SCIENCE OF NUMBERS

***

One morning, Imani's sister Nina came to her house. Imani was preparing for a business meeting so I answered the door and Nina, who looked vibrant and energetic, came in saying that she had a dream about Imani the night before and she came over to make sure everything was alright. She said the dream was giving her two numbers, a six and a two. When I hear anything with numbers I reflect to one of the lessons given by the Honorable Elijah Muhammad that stated that every number had significance except the number eight (except that it is a multiple of four). I could not figure out what the significance of the numbers meant at the time but I later studied a bit more and found that the numbers Nina had dreamt of were very significant.

Imani's numbers seem to be the "three" and the "four". Three's and four's always came up for her. Three is the number that represents "a trial" (tri means three) and four represents "foundation" (four legs to a table or chair).

Let me list a few things here to help you understand:

- Nina dreamt of a *six*, which is a multiple of *three.* She also dreamt of a *two.* If you add *two* plus *six*, you will get *eight*, which is a multiple of *four.* (also, remember the day that I taped Imani in the Park was February 26th)

This is not an attempt to get anyone "spooked out". I am merely saying that all of these facts help to make up some of Imani's spiral of life and that she was destined to be a very enlightened spiritual being.

I knew that Imani and I meeting and getting to know each other over the course of about six months was no accident. I believe she came into my life to provide much needed instruction and character for use in my own life or to pass on to others. The number representing a trial (three) and the number representing foundation (four) were around us also. Again, the numbers bear me witness:

- Our first meeting and talk was on 10/22/01 (the numbers added together equal six which is a multiple of three)
- Our last day together was 4/15/02 (the numbers equal twenty-one, and two plus one equals three)
- We were joined together for a total of 175 days (the numbers equal 13, and one plus four equals four).
- We were both 40 years of age on October 22, 2001 (remember the significance of 40)
- We were both 22 years out of high school (the numbers added equal four)

Trials and tests were all around Imani and now the energy and power of those same trials also engulfed me. THE GOOD NEWS IS THAT HER NUMBERS, THE THREE AND THE FOUR, ADDED TOGETHER GIVE US SEVEN, AND SEVEN IS THE NUMBER OF PERFECTION! Just ask Stevie Wonder, the "Eighth" wonder of the world or Erykah Badu, who named her son "Seven". By the way, Imani even wore a size seven shoe.

The more I look at the two numbers that Nina dreamt about, the more I realize just how powerful our energy is. As Imani always said, we have the power to send messages out into the universe, and others persons, if spiritually awakened, have the power to receive those same messages.

# 18.
# READING THE SIGNS

***

On April 6, 2002 we went to New York to spend the day. We went to Harlem first and had lunch at a Caribbean restaurant on 125th Street near Lenox Avenue. Imani had fish with rice and beans. My stomach was a little "busted" so I didn't really want to eat anything. I picked a little from her plate. After lunch, we walked down 125th Street doing a little shopping along the way. Imani was looking for some sandals but didn't really see any that she liked. I wanted to treat her to the sandals but I remember thinking about the old saying that says "be careful when you buy someone shoes, because they may walk out of your life". THIS PROVED TO BE MORE THAN JUST A SAYING!

It was chilly out but we walked up a few blocks to the Krispy Creme doughnut store. Imani wasn't about to leave Harlem without making that stop! Of course, I, once again, had to "cut up" a little once we got into the store. I began asking people for a bite of their doughnut that they were eating. I was trying to confirm what I told Imani .... "Krispy Crème is a cult". We got a good laugh as one older woman agreed with me that Dunkin Doughnuts were just as good. Her daughter, who looked at me like I was certifiably crazy when I asked for a bite of her doughnut was too busy gobbling up her own doughnut to join in the conversation. We left and we decided to ride to mid-town and watch a movie. Imani and I both wanted a future that included a good amount of traveling. Imani actually wanted residences in New York, Maryland and California. As we rode through mid-town she said "see that building over there?" She went on, "Mariah Carey, has one like it and lives on, I believe, the 17th floor". Imani said that she also wanted to live on one of the higher floors. She wanted to reside in the various states for a few months out of the year to share her spiritual gifts. We also talked about going to Africa in the year 2003, together.

We had seen just about everything that was out but I really wanted to see a foreign film that I had read a preview about called "Y Tu Mama Tambien", which I believe translates into "And Me too Mama also". The reviews said it was a very good movie. It was in Spanish with English subtitles. Imani was a little skeptical but agreed to go. The theater was on 42nd Street near 8th Avenue. We kept up with reading the subtitles and really enjoyed this movie. It was a funny story about two young guys who went on an adventure with a woman who ended up teaching them about life and love even though she knew her own life would end shortly thereafter due to some type of cancer. She, by her presence and interaction allowed them to learn about some of their innermost feelings. Had she not spiraled into their lives, they may not have ever learned the things they learned as a result of her being with them. The part about her dying was sad but overall we laughed a lot and was in such a good mood we decided to watch another movie called Amelie'.

The movie Amelie' movie was also a foreign film with English subtitles. This was the first time in my life that I had ever seen two foreign films in a row. It was about a woman who got enjoyment when she helped others get together. Amelie' helped spread love in her own special and unique way.

It is so fitting, as I look back at the two movies we saw that night, that the two movies were about people who seemed to have a distinct purpose in life which included teaching others about love. This is so close to what Imani always said of herself. That SHE WAS BORN TO LOVE. In retrospect, it now appears that the selection of movies that night was no coincidence.

## 19.
## THE PATIENT WAIT

***

On April 13th, I was hanging in Plainfield with my partner Antoine Roney. "Toine", as I call him, and I go way back. He is one of my true friends and is really like a brother to me. We were hanging around Brother Bill's barbershop on West Fourth Street. Brother Bill is an entrepreneur, owning real estate and a barbershop. He also has a health food store across the street from the barbershop, which also carries a few books. I bought a Holy Qu'ran for Imani. She had gone away to Maryland to coach at Iyanla Van Zant's school, so since I had time on my hands, I rode down to Neptune and Asbury Park to check out some property that was for sale. I looked at some of the commercial property thinking that it would make a nice Spiritual Center for Imani. I told her that I would help her build a spiritual empire. When I got back, I stopped in Plainfield since it was still early. Bill was telling me that he and his wife may be sponsoring a trip to Africa. He went on to tell me that he owned property in Ghana and that he was having a large home built there.

I gave Bill my business card and said to him that I would like him to reserve two spaces and I would like to start paying on the trip this year. After this talk with Bill, I felt it was meant to be that Imani and I go. It was so odd that I was even in Plainfield, especially on a Saturday. Saturday had become "me and Imani's day". This had become the day that I would get whatever work I had to do over with early, so I could spend some quality time with my sweetie. It was always "quality" time. I was really just waiting patiently for Imani to get back in town.

I ran into a long time friend, Naheem, who passed by the barbershop that day. Naheem is one of the first brothers to begin teaching me Islam. He is one of those highly intelligent brothers that has yet to utilize his full potential due to the magnetism of the street life. We were going to Hubbard School and were just in 6th or 7th grade but Naheem's message was simple, yet different. He would tell us to "STOP EATING THAT PORK!". His message helped me begin my transformation. I began reading more and more literature concerning Islam even though my father was against it. I told Naheem that Imani told me she had ran into him not long ago and that she said he seemed to be doing fine.

Imani called me on Sunday to say she was heading home from Maryland. She expected to be home by 9:00 P.M. I told her not to rush and I would talk to her later. I told her I missed her and that I would take off from work to spend time with her the following day. She said she missed me too but felt she would not be good company because she would be tired. Imani always needed a day to recuperate after her weekend in Maryland.

When she called me later, she wanted to know if I was definitely coming to her house the next day. Imani always wanted to know for sure. A "maybe" wasn't good enough. Not only did she want a definite yes or no, but she also wanted to know the time. If I said I would be there at 11:00 A.M. and didn't make it there at that time for some reason, then at 11: 05 A.M., I would get a call asking me where I was. I was always pretty good with my timing. I assured her that I would be there in the morning but I made sure I didn't pinpoint a specific time because I knew she would hold me to it. I was anxious to see her so I knew I would handle a few things in the morning and make my way to her house as quickly as I could.

# 20.
# THE DAY OF PEACE

***

On Monday, April 15, 2002, I arrived at Imani's house about 10:30 A.M. I had bought her the Holy Qu'ran and a movie called "Changing Lanes" starring Samuel Jackson and Ben Affleck. Imani looked very relaxed wearing a yellow and orange tie-dyed, long skirt and one yellow and one orange tank top. She looked beautiful. We were definitely in relax mode. She told me about her weekend in Maryland. She told me of an incident with her roommate, who invited another woman to also share their hotel room. The woman stated that she was too tired to drive home for the night and the hotel was completely booked. Imani felt that the situation should have been presented to her earlier and felt somewhat violated. She said that she would get her own space in the future even though it meant paying additional fees. She said the peace and contentment would be worth it. We popped the tape in and began watching the movie but we may have both dozed off once or twice before it was over. She was still tired from her weekend and I was just in a very relaxed state of being.

After the movie, Imani suggested we have lunch delivered. She knew about a place not far away that we could order the food. I agreed and she ordered one her favorite dishes. It was a grilled chicken salad. I ordered eggplant parmesan, which ended up being the wrong choice. Certain dishes, you can't order from just anywhere. Imani shared her salad, so I was okay. After lunch we relaxed some more, we talked about life and love, we bonded, we listened to music, we laughed and we expressed our love for each other. It was a great day! It was the type of day that you would want to live everyday. What we experienced that day could be described as pure peace! We departed that day saying the exact same words to each other, ….."I LOVE YOU". Those words were not strange to us. We had grown to a point where we used those words regularly. We are not promised tomorrow, and I believe that if there are people in your life who you love, it is important to let them know that you love them. I am now trying to incorporate that action more and more in my life.

I left between 5:00 P.M. and 5:30 P.M. and headed to Orange to pick up my children, Asia and Omar. I called Imani when I got to Orange to let her know I was back. I never felt funny or intimidated about calling to let her know I was back. Some guys think they are acting "soft" if they call their girlfriend to say they have made it back home safely. It felt natural and I was always secure with my manhood so it was not a problem. I think that's one of the things that made Imani feel comfortable with me. She always gave me that same respect.

## 21.
## YELLOW SANDALS

***

The next day during my lunch hour I went to a shoe store to get my children some shoes. While I was in the store I began looking at the women's shoes. I saw a pair of yellow sandals that were a size seven. It was the last pair they had. I don't recall having any thoughts that maybe I shouldn't buy them because as the saying goes, "she may walk out of my life". I didn't even think about the significance of the color yellow and how it represents friendship, probably because my lunch hour always seems like the fastest hour of the day. I guess I was still thinking about the beautiful orange and yellow outfit Imani had on the day before and I figured she would like the sandals. I had to get them. That night I decided I would ride out to Piscataway and give them to her. Going to see her on a Tuesday would have been out of the ordinary due to my schedule usually not allowing this. I finished up some work about 8:30 P.M. and started on my way. I began calling her cell phone to let her know I was coming, but did not get an answer. Even though we had grown very close, I didn't just pop up at her house and she didn't just pop up at mine. It was a common respect that we had for each other.

She normally got home about 9:15 P.M. on Tuesday's. I started calling the home number but also got no answer. By about 9:20 P.M. when I had still not received a response to my calls I left a message on her machine saying that I was going to come to see her but because I got no answer I was turning around and going back home. I figured she would call me at some point that night and say she got backed up with work or that she had a client that needed to speak to her, and it took up a lot of time. I could remember certain times when I was there with her, even though she was tired, if she received a telephone call from someone who expressed that they really needed her counseling, then she would make the call rather then put it off until the next day. It is a true act of charity when you sacrifice yourself for the benefit of someone else. Knowing these things, I was patient but I never received the call.

# 22.
# AGONY AND PAIN

***

The next morning, I noticed a call had come through on my cell phone but I had missed the call. The number had a "908" area code and I did not recognize the number. I tried calling the number back but the line was busy. When I got to work, I tried the number a few times but each time it was busy. About 10:00 A.M., I received a call from Imani's brother Craig. I figured quickly in my mind that this was the strange number on my cell phone and that Imani must be sick or in the hospital. THE NEWS WAS MUCH WORSE THAN THAT. Craig DROPPED IT ON ME QUICKLY, … Imani IS DEAD! I'm not sure if those were his exact words but that is the message that my mind received. I said "WHAT?" , even though I knew I heard what he said. I threw the telephone to the floor and cried out so loud that many of my co-workers came running over to my desk. I had my head down and was crying uncontrollably. I got myself somewhat together and got back on the phone. I told Craig that I would make my way to Plainfield, to his mother's house.

I drove to Plainfield with tears streaming down my face and my heart began burning. I called my friend Toine because I felt that I needed some type of support in facing this dramatic turn of events. I picked him up and we rode to Imani's mother's house. Upon our arrival, I saw a white butterfly flying around the house. It was the first butterfly I had seen all year. At that same time Antoine commented saying that THE BUTTERFLY WAS SOME TYPE OF BLESSING. My mind did not reflect, at that time, to the very spiritual conversation I had with Imani that chilly night at B.B. Kings in New York when she mentioned that if she was reincarnated she wanted to come back as a butterfly. I went into the house and upon seeing Mrs. Cole, I again lost control of my emotions once again. I'm sure I wet her shirt up pretty good. Even though I saw all of the people sitting around in the house, I was still waiting for Imani to walk out of some back room and say that it was all a big joke. The mind is something!

Craig told me some of the things that happened that led to Imani's physical departure. They were playing tennis the day before for two to three hours in the hot sun. That day the temperature was in the mid-90's. Imani didn't particularly like drinking water.

I needed to know what happened. I needed more answers. I began calling the hospital to get details on when Imani was picked up and how long it took the ambulance to get to the hospital. I wanted to be sure that everyone did what they were supposed to do. I knew that would not bring my sweetie back but I felt I had to do it, probably for my own sanity.

The days that followed were terrible for me. I was in pure agony going through what most people go through at times like these. I wrestled with thoughts of guilt saying that things would have been different had I been there. I missed Imani so much and now realized just how much I loved her. I knew I loved her and told her regularly, but I didn't know how much. I didn't want to stay by myself so I spent nights at my brother Michael's house at night and went to the Cole's house during the day. I knew I wasn't going back to work until after the funeral. I hardly slept. I prayed much and talking to God and to Imani every night. I cried many nights hoping that Imani would somehow come back to me. In the final analysis I realized that physical death is final and that Imani would live on forever in me and in others. It was a hard pill to swallow but I knew I had to do it.

## 23.
## ABOVE ALL THY GETTING

***

I had to understand that Imani's life and the lessons she had been given and tried to give to others were divine. I had to realize that her "mission" was bigger than me. Imani said that the most important relationship we have is our relationship with God. Imani said that we must all learn to tell the truth. She said she had a problem with white people in particular because they had deceived so many people with lies that affect so many generations. The effects of those lies have been perpetuated and passed down through many families. The descendents of those same white people have benefited greatly and should therefore take on the responsibility of re-educating the masses of people. She also said that we must learn to forgive. She said if we don't forgive then we keep the problem within our own vessel but if we forgive it allows the universe a chance to provide justice. She said we must learn how to trust. She said trust in God because God is in all that exist. She recognized that we all, including herself, had to constantly work on these things in order to elevate to the higher levels of consciousness.

The days that followed were still filled with agony and pain. The wake came about one week later. I hardly slept in between. I didn't go to work. I was just "out of it"! I went to the barbershop one day to talk to my friend, who is more like a brother, Gerard Abdul, who cuts hair to finance his aspiring music and producing careers. His side kick is Zeke Brown, a veteran barber who has also become a father figure to Gerard. I told him my sad news, but since he never really knew the height of the relationship, he couldn't console me. He did provide strength, however, with his normal "oh well, life goes on attitude," when I told him what happened. I was probably looking for some form of piety but instead I got a message that basically translates into 'SUCK IT UP MAN AND KEEP GOING'. It's funny how strength comes to us sometimes in packages we don't immediately recognize.

# 24.
# LOVING SUPPORT

***

I was so surprised when I went to pick up Gina Goode, a long time friend of Imani's, at the Newark airport and she had arranged to have my sister Mary fly in from Atlanta with her. I could never thank Gina enough for helping to get Mary to New Jersey to be with me. I was surprised and felt a lot better when I saw her. The Cole family had handled most of the business that needed to be handled. I helped out wherever I could. So many people came out to the wake. I mean thousands of people from every walk of life came to honor this woman. Most that came out probably did not know of Imani's spiritual advancements and achievements. I saw people that I hadn't seen in over thirty years. I figured it was because I hadn't lived in Plainfield since 1983 but others who never left the City stated later that everybody, who hadn't been seen for years, had crawled from under every rock to make it out to this wake. I felt honored for Imani. I didn't feel ready to go see her body at the start of the wake so I just took a seat. My sister Mary and my brother Joe, were with me throughout the whole ordeal. I really appreciate and love them for that.

My brother Mike and his fiancé Kiesha also came to the wake. The presence and support of my family and friends helped me tremendously. I did finally go up to the casket at the end of the wake to look at a collage of photos that had been put together by some of Imani's family. I also looked at the body of Imani and I said a prayer asking God to allow her spirit to live on in others. The feeling of great pain and great loss began to elevate within me. I cried again before leaving and going back to the Cole's home. I stayed there not knowing where else to go. I stayed up late that night talking and bonding with Imani's father, Mr. Cole. I think he felt my pain also, and knew I really needed someone to talk to.

Even as I tell this story, the tears swell in my eyes because to this day I still really, really miss Imani. What we had was so new, but it also had so much promise. We never had an argument. If we disagreed about something, we discussed it.

## 25.
## GIVING HONOR

***

The next day was the funeral. I had stayed in Plainfield that night at my brother Mike's home but forgot my black shoes, so I had to ride back to Newark to get them. I was nervous. I didn't know what to wear. I think I finally decided to wear my navy blue pinstripe suit. Imani did a chart on me once and she told me to wear a lot of blue. Imani's spirit was on me heavily that day. I wanted things to be right for her. I began thinking about the mints that Imani used to keep. She loved those peppermint lifesavers, and always seemed to have a big supply of them in her house and in her car. Also, as a Muslim, I had been taught that a mint taken in the mouth and melting represents the physical body going away but the sweet memories of the person remaining behind. I had to get some mints for the people who would come to the funeral. I told Mrs. Cole that I wanted to get to the church early to make sure everything was okay.

I was feeling Imani's spirit in everything that I did. I spread out the mints on two tables in the foyer of the church. I went to speak to the Ministers in the church to see if there was any outstanding financial obligations that were due. It seemed they didn't quite understand my connection or motives. That didn't matter to me. I was attempting to do all of the things Imani would want me to do in that situation. Imani would want everyone involved, properly compensated and she would want to be represented in a distinguished manner. I pray that this was handled correctly.

I had been writing down some things about Imani over the last few days that I wanted to say at her funeral. I didn't want to do it for any vain purpose or to try to project anything of falsehood. I wanted to speak to the people who cared about Imani and those who loved her, and let them know that she had been happy at this particular time in her life. She was enjoying her life though she sometimes complained of terrible headaches. I felt Imani wanted me to speak and represent her. I believe that if it had been my body lying in that casket instead of hers, that she would have done the same for me.

It's funny that a guy like me, who unconsciously prides himself in being immune to the devastating events that go on in the world, hardly ever cries unless very deeply touched. I had a conversation with Bilal, a few days later and he said "BROTHER, I NEVER CRY...BUT WHEN I HEARD ABOUT Imani, TEARS CAME DOWN MY FACE". I could only shake my head in agreement as I understood exactly what he was saying.

I still pray and ask that the spirit of Imani live on in me and in others. I look at her face everyday. I know she will always be with me. I will always miss her physical presence but I will continue to seek more understanding regarding the timing of her departure. I could not and would not, judge Imani and the life she led before I really met her. She told me about things she had done in the past but that is not for me to judge. My judgements are limited to the times that we were able to share and the work I saw her involved in. We, as sinners should be careful about how we judge others, especially if the judgement is based on past activities. How about those individuals, male or female, Christian, Muslim, Jewish or otherwise, who have committed a crime and served their sentence. After serving their time, they begin leading a life of saving souls and lives! How would you judge them?

If that example is too drastic, how about the Minister or Imam, who used to hang out in bars BEFORE they chose to serve in those roles, which come with great responsibility.

I just recently had a conversation with a Christian minister who said to me that some people had a problem with him because they say how much he used to hang out. I told him that he was probably better equipped to deal with many of the issues that come up. I also said that "YOU CAN'T APPRECIATE LIFE UNTIL YOU'VE TASTED DEATH"! I deal with people based on my own communication with them. I don't care what others may say about someone, especially without proof. Anyone who knows me would bear witness to that. I don't care if the whole city is against you, I will not turn against you based on what others say.

JESUS FASTED FOR *FORTY* DAYS. IN THE DAYS OF NOAH, IT RAINED FOR *FORTY* DAYS AND THE HONORABLE ELIJAH MUHAMMAD SAID HE WOULD CLIMB A MOUNTAIN *FORTY* MILES HIGH, JUST TO TEACH ONE.

I am not attempting to put Imani on the same level as these great prophets and messengers but what I am saying is that you never know what kind of sacrifice it takes to save people. Now, it just so happens that Imani was here among us for FORTY years. It could be that it also took Imani that long…or, it took that much of a sacrifice, just to save *one.* That "one" could be me or any reader of this book. That "one" could also be an unborn child who directly or indirectly is touched or transformed by any of Imani's words, *or* it could have been

Imani herself. YES, YOU CAN SAVE YOURSELF! (God, of course is in control).

My goal now, is to incorporate into my life some of the lessons that Imani taught about trust, truth and forgiveness. I received a revelation of getting a memorial erected for Imani at the tennis court near her home, where family and friends could visit for years to come. That is now one of my missions. The proceeds of this book will assist in the realization of that mission. It would be very fitting since she played her last games there. The phrase "40 Love" used in the scoring of tennis, now has more meaning to me than ever before. SHE WAS FORTY AND SHE WAS BORN TO LOVE.

***

Yes, I will move on in my life because Imani would want me to. I believe Imani would want all those who love her, and also those who now know of her through the reading of this book, to learn from her existence and practice divine principles that bring us closer to God.

***

**AS I SAID AT THE FUNERAL, Imani IS NOT DEAD. SHE WILL LIVE ON IN ME AND IN ALL THOSE THAT LOVE HER.**

***

(ETERNITY HAS NO END)

# EPILOGUE

***

This writing was part of a self imposed mission of sorts to not only memorialize my loving friend but to also provide healing to my own soul. I experienced various emotional changes, of course, in completing this project. I had to carry on the daily functions of going to work everyday, picking up my children after work, taking them home to fix their evening meal, bathing them and finally putting them to bed. After that vigorous schedule I would then attempt to collect my thoughts and muster up enough energy to sit in front of the computer and begin pecking away until my mind drew a blank. Many times I would pray for energy and assistance. I prayed to Allah (God) to sustain me so that I may complete this part project. I now thank Him that He allowed me to do just that. The other part of this project and mission is to have a memorial erected in Imani's honor near the tennis courts where she played shortly before she passed on.

My attempt through this writing was not selfish however. I did not merely want to relay some distant story to the reader that they could not internalize, but instead I wanted the reader to develop a connection to the spiritual and motivational aspects of this writing. My hopes were that the reader would do a self-analysis of some of the ways they handle relationships, their own spiritual well being, and their connection with God.

I prefaced my writing by first attempting to establish the concept of predetermined destiny and how certain lives are spiraled into other certain lives not by accident but rather by interconnectivity that is built into the universal order of things, much like prophecy being fulfilled.

I included much information about my own upbringing to paint a picture of why a life like my own would draw a person that had developed into such a spiritual being at such a pivotal time in my life.

Through our experiences with our families, neighbors and the "village", as I described in this book, we develop a sense of who we are, and as we grow in awareness we begin to recognize what areas that we excel in as well as the areas that we are deficient.

In the midst of trying to determine who we are and what we will ultimately become, many of us surrounded by a steady stream of opportunities take the wrong path, begin to wage a major war of good versus evil. I often refer to this period of time as "the fork in he road". This is that point where you come to and you have to make a serious decision whether you will do right or wrong and you know your decision will impact how you spend the rest of your life. My friends that took the wrong path in life know exactly what I am talking about.

I came to those same crossroads while I was still young. I had made a conscious decision that there would be a place that I would draw the line. Even though, I would continue doing things that were not perfect and other things that were easily construed as being evil, there were some things that I just would not do. In some instances, in seams that the "crossroads" are endless and we continue to get the opportunity to make the right choice. In other cases it appears that we will never have that choice again.

In writing about our meeting of the minds in "elevated places" and the protocol of "three dimensional bonding", I attempted to convey the success two people can have when they prioritize their levels of communication with each other and first establish a spiritual connection, second, find a comfortable and communicative mental level, and third, manifest their physical attraction for each other. Even though it is usually the physical attraction that initiates the process, it should not be permitted to dominate and become the main focus. When spirituality is made the number one priority it keeps the mind elevated and therefore the communication on a high level. Where the mind goes the body will follow.

There was a great contrast in our lives especially when you look at the "mother" factor. She had that influence constantly while I did not. Instead I used a combination of various women including my grandmother, neighborhood mothers, teachers and ultimately my own mother to obtain a certain level of motherly comfort to sustain me until I reached adulthood.

I put Imani's actual words in this book so the reader can dissect the words for themselves. Educators and students alike agree that upon looking at something more than once and reading something over and over again, you usually get something more out of it that differs from the previous time. She had a message for the world and she delivered it in fine fashion. She also had words for me that remain crucial to my constant battle to uplift my own spirituality.

I expressed the happiness and joy we both experienced when we shared our space with each other. Some people live their entire lives and never find a person that they can connect with on such a high spiritual level and at other times just laugh and have fun. We shared great conversations that touched on so many different subject matters but never argued even if we disagreed. The lesson and instruction to those who read this material, who may be having trouble in these areas is to keep the level of respect up on the highest level. That respect will allow both parties to listen carefully when the other person is speaking and insure that ego's don't get in the way of progress.

There is also a mathematical element that brings about cycles. Historically, we will find that men and women come on the scene and leave. Some of those same men and women came as a prototype or sign of another one coming behind them as an act of fulfillment of that sign. This is a much harder school of thought to study and master because the prototype or sign could appear one thousand years before the actual fulfillment it or they could appear one day before the fulfillment of it.

I expressed being patient but having the desire to be with someone for all of the right reasons, always yielding to any selfish thoughts. In the chapter entitled "The Day of Peace" I wanted to paint a picture of a day of pure peace and contentment. Days when you can take a deep, deep breathe and relax as though you are on a beautiful vacation, are indeed within our reach if the correct chemistry has been developed and maintained.

Joy and pain seem to share the same spectrum even though they are on opposite ends. Much like the comparison of love and hate being two emotions but they travel in different directions as they intensify. The pain that people experience in life have a direct correlation to the joy they also have been exposed to. It's almost like the famous saying that goes… the bigger they are…the harder they fall. Well, the bigger your love experience is, the deeper the pain will be when comes to an end. When we experience agony and pain, it is actually a wake up message to say that we are vulnerable to our own emotions. This is not necessarily a bad thing, but instead it is a human thing that we should come to grips with. We can, at these critical and crucial times pull away much understanding and many lessons about life itself.

In times of instability when we feel we may not be able to cope with a given situation, our support systems kick in. This support system made up of our family and friends are directed to us by the energy in the universe answering our call for assistance and also by God Himself as he answers our sincere prayers.

Going through such trials is likened to climbing a high mountain and not being sure you can do it. As we our bought over to the other side of the mountain and plant our feet once again on safe ground, we gain a new sense of our abilities and who we are deep down inside.

The final chapter called "Giving Honor" was written to say that it is fine to honor someone's life after they are physically gone but it is even more important to honor them while they are among us. We should all live by that simple rule... "do unto others as you would have other's do unto you". The slave-holders, the so-called founding father's of this country, those that seek to rape and rob the earth of it's riches and many, many of us today, have yet to learn and incorporate this lesson.

When you complete the reading of this book, you should be more willing and able to conduct a relationship that is filled with spirituality, patience, honor and respect. Read the words that Imani provided in the Chapter entitled "She Spoke to the World" and use her words as a blueprint. If you seek these things you must begin with an earnest attempt to work on yourself, constantly, to cleanse your soul and purify your heart.

I am doing the same and consider myself to be "a work in progress". I pray for your success.

I thank those that have contributed to my development in all areas. I especially thank AllAh (God) for allowing Imani Amour to come to me and inspire my life.

HE INDEED SENT ME AN ANGEL.

***

***



Imani often told me that I was "some kinda' special" and

I always felt that that phrase fit her even more so I wrote and gave her this poem to explain what I meant.

***

## SOME KINDA' SPECIAL

You are "Some Kinda' Special" even though
you describe me that way,
I am so engrossed by your spirituality
and the things you have to say
You are definitely connected to the higher
power of God,
That spirit pulsates inside you and is alive
like Moses' rod
The path that you are on could only lead
to Heaven on Earth,
Your integrity and character have proven
to have real worth
You are "Some Kinda' Special"
so I borrowed those words from you,
Your Divine protocol is in order and
I feel your heart is true
Let me change gears .... and ask you
(all my life) where have you been?
Oh yeah... you were busy tastin' death while
I was busy tastin' sin
We both had turmoil in our lives doing things
that could've taken away our breath
They say... you can't appreciate life
until you've tasted death.
Your Some Kinda' Special,
spiritually high and doing fine,

Your ready for your future and
your mate that is divine.
You'll be like Hagar being directed to
"Zam Zam" by an Angel,
Then you'll drink of life and tie a knot,
only God could untangle.
Peace.

***



***

## AUTHOR'S BIOGRAPHY

*Angelo Omar*

Attended Plainfield High School and Kean College in Union, New Jersey. Joined the Nation of Islam in 1978 in Plainfield New Jersey.

He has three children Tariq, Asia and Omar and also portrays a fatherly role to Malcolm Roan and his goddaughter Laeequa Nelson. He invests in both residential and commercial real estate.

In May of 1995 he joined the City of Newark as the Specification Writer. A former staff writer for "Visions-Weekly" Newspaper. He also writes poetry and songs.

Owns and operates A-1 Video Production and Photography. Also check website at www.a1videoproduction.com

## FULL BOOK REVIEWS

***

"Spectacular! Brilliant! Forceful! A compelling story told with such sincerity and candor that it will lift you up and transport you to a world where you will discover that truth, honesty and fearlessness are the keys to freedom. I MET AN ANGEL" soars like a butterfly".

"A story of love, growth and transformation that brought tears to my eyes and made my heart skip a beat! It had me recalling the days of my youth with joy and a smile on my face. A milestone among great books that free the mind and fills the spirit. A milestone and destined to be and true BESTSELLER among the new school of heart to heart non-fiction forms".

Edward "Jockey" Anderson, Author
*They Must have had Wings*

***

"It was actually good reading. I'm quite impressed honestly and that's not so easy to do".

Julius Tajiddin
Soul Biz Online - Book Review

***

"I Met An Angel is a must read autobiographical love story (post memoir) of a man (Angelo Omar) who finally meets the woman (Imani) he wants to spend the rest of his life with after knowing her for over 20 years. And just as miraculously as she came back into his life, this time as a soul mate, like an Angel completing her mission, their physical journey together suddenly ends but their spiritual journey continues".

***

I Met An Angel by Angelo Omar
Reviewed by Edward Hawthorne

***

This book is a fundraising effort to raise money to erect a memorial. All donations are appreciated and may be sent to A-1 Video Production at 4300 Yeager Road, Douglasville, GA 30135.

***